TORN PAGES

BLOOD & INK

VOLUME ONE

ASHLEY CHAPMAN

WOLF AND ROSE PUBLISHING

ISBNs
EBook: 978-1-964977-00-3
Paperback: 978-1-964977-01-0
Hardcover: -

Cover by Rae Sawyer

For Aunt Deb, the first book for the first person to believe in my writing

CONTENTS

INTRODUCTION

Torn Pages is a cozy urban fantasy romance between a socially anxious author and an emotionally repressed vampire politician. This book aims to tell a heartwarming story, but does include elements that may not be suitable for some. Mentions of **prejudice**, **anxiety**, **depression**, and **stalking** (not in relation to our love interests) are present in the novel. Also, this book contains soul-crushingly anxious interactions, so if you are are sensitive to second hand embarrassment, reader be warned.

CHAPTER 1

><<>Mr. DeVito<><>

*A*fternoon sunbeams drifted through the floor-to-ceiling windows of the HOME office. But they were the only lazy elements of the building's atmosphere. Pens tapped, feet shuffled, and a low buzz dominated the air. It wasn't the air conditioning: the staff was on edge. Every television in every room blared the same headline:

"Vampire and Werewolf Attacks That Result in Turning Could Be Reclassified as Murder Under New Proposed Law."

To those who worked for Help to Obtain Monster Equality (HOME), it was a crisis in the making.

"It's bad enough that we haven't been able to convince the legislature that attacks by starved or unmedicated supernaturals should qualify for an insanity plea," grumbled Luna, a pale, blonde werewolf, as she leaned against the hallway wall and stared moodily at her drink. "If these were humans we were talking about, it wouldn't be a debate. But because it's supernaturals, nobody cares!"

Her work wife Erin, a raven-haired and dark-skinned witch, nodded gravely. "Did you hear what else is in the proposal? They're pushing for spells that go wrong or potions with negative side-effects to be punishable by law. As if half the drugs passed by the FDA don't have worse side-effects than any potion I've ever heard of!" Erin smashed the paper cup she had been drinking from and slammed it in the trash. "And there's a rumor of requiring every shapeshifter to register their DNA with the government, too!"

Before Luna could reply, the two women were brushed aside by HOME President, Stella Melburne. She was an imposing dark elf whose presence took up far more space than her physical stature. Most days she would have stopped to chat with the other women, but today her violet eyes burned and she moved with purpose.

And behind her was the tall, slender form of vampire Reuben DeVito. His slicked-back black hair without a single strand out of place stood in stark contrast to his snowy white skin. The crisp shirt and well-tailored suit he wore revealed how utterly thin he was, while leaving little of his sallow skin visible.

Despite his sharp features and equally sharp frown, there was a softness in the vampire's eyes that still managed to put those around him at ease. He nodded briefly at the gossiping pair as he passed, then disappeared into the office at the end of the hall.

"Woah," whispered Luna, staring at the closed door. "Even in a time like this, Vampire Vito comes in here looking immaculate! I swear I've never seen so much as a smudge on his shoe!"

Erin snickered and lightly punched her friend's shoulder. "There's a reason he's the HOME rep, Lu. And if I didn't know better, I'd think you had a crush on him."

In the office at the end of the hall, Mr. DeVito stood at perfect attention in front of Stella's desk. The only sign of any discomfort was the way he fidgeted with the cuff of his sleeve with his two middle fingers. He didn't say a word as Stella settled into her chair and flipped open the file folder she had been carrying.

"No doubt you've heard the headlines and know what they mean for us," the elf said, gesturing to a chair to Mr. DeVito's left. "Sit."

With no hesitation, he perched on the edge of the seat, back ramrod straight and eyes still focused on his manager. *We're Mr. DeVito right now. Calm face. Steady hands. Eye contact. Professional.*

"The PR department sent out a poll early this morning as soon as the news broke, and the results are as bad as we could've imagined. You've dropped ten percent in the polls as of 9AM, and the downward trend doesn't seem to be slowing down. All this talk of attacks has the humans up in arms."

A flash of fear crossed Mr. DeVito's face and he wanted to ask Stella what could be done about the issue, but seeing that she still had her 'rant ahead' face on, he choked back his words and fidgeted with a crease in his pants.

And rant on she did. "Things are stable in the outer limits of the city where the population is mostly supernatural, but the human-heavy city center polls are worrying. And the suburbs, well. Apparently the mixed numbers of supernaturals and humans are allowing the viral headlines to hit even harder there."

Stella leaned back in her chair with her leg draped over her knee, the red stiletto she wore bouncing with irritation. "You've dropped to a 22% approval rating because of all the fearmongering going on. I'm still waiting for the polls outside Beaumont to come in."

"The elections are way too close for controversy like this..." Mr. DeVito finally said. "And the supernatural community has too much at stake."

"Indeed. You, perhaps better than anyone else, know how precarious our position is and how important HOME is to the supernaturals we serve. It's imperative that we get your voice, and by extension the voice of supernaturals, into the legislature. We can't survive on donations anymore. We need government funding, we need community support, and we need to show humanity that we are not monsters. And we *don't* need any more laws that will result in more loss of supernatural lives!"

Stella's stern eyes softened, but only for a split second. "Humanity has never made supernatural welfare the top of their priority list. I thought we were making progress in the sixty years since we were granted citizenship, but today's headlines have proven me wrong. It seems they're still set on punishing instead of helping, and othering instead of embracing. We need to remind them that supernaturals are people too."

Mr. DeVito frowned. "Concessions are expensive and we still aren't seen as a priority. Even though we go to great lengths to create supernatural soup kitchens, distribute medications, and provide homes, and not just for supernaturals, it's never enough! We've come a long way in combating the social injustices we face, but there's still a long way to go. And humanity can't seem to see that we're helping them, too."

"Indeed. It's not fair, but all we can do is keep fighting."

Mr. DeVito nodded, but did not reply. He was the do-er of the plans, not the planner of the plans, so the fact that Stella had called him in meant she already had *something* up her sleeve. For a moment he wished that his vampirism had given him mind-reading abilities, but alas. He was a supernatural, not a superhero.

He was, however, correct.

"We do have a plan, but it will rely on you and your ability to maintain the public persona you've spent the last decade cultivating with us. And perhaps a bit of acting." Stella's foot dropped to the floor and she leaned over the desk to open the mysterious folder. After flipping a few pages, she spun the whole thing around and pushed it toward Mr. DeVito.

He looked down and for the first time since the door closed, his expression changed from blank to confusion. "This…is an application to the yearly HOME speed dating event."

"Yes, yes it is."

"And…how is this supposed to help me win back the voters?"

Stella stared at Mr. DeVito, giving a tisk of disgust. "You're going to attend the event and find a human to date publicly. It doesn't really matter if you end up together or not. Your goal is to get someone to spend time with you in public, and be convincing enough that the public sees that a supernatural and a human can coexist. Show them your humanity." The grin which spread across her face could almost be described as 'wicked' as Mr. DeVito digested the information.

It was the stupidest plan he'd ever heard in his entire life.

But before he allowed his tongue to take the lead, he changed the words on their way out. "I see. If that's what it takes, then I'll give it a try."

"You won't *try*. You'll make it happen like you always do. You've been around long enough to remember a world without HOME. We can't backslide."

Just the insinuation was enough to cause the vampire's insides to quake.

"You're right, like you always are. Give me the form and I'll have it back to you by the end of the day."

The smile on Stella's face widened further, but then grew solemn. "Good boy. There's one other thing we need to discuss before you go, though. We have received another round of threats this morning. I really think it's time that you accept the offer of a security detail. You were lucky to avoid the brawl that broke out in front of the HOME building last week, but you can't always rely on luck."

"I wouldn't actually be in danger. I'm not afraid of a group of frightened humans. Worst case I just use my vampiric speed to zip away."

Stella's frown grew deeper and she shook her head. "You don't understand, Mr. DeVito. Multiple of the arrested protestors had syringes of vampire serum in their possession. And we don't know where they are getting it."

"...Vampire serum? You mean the stuff they use for the death penalty?!" If Mr. DeVito had any color in his face, it would have drained. He sat back in his chair with fear dimming his eyes as Stella nodded.

"I'm sure I don't have to warn you what would happen if one of them managed to inject you with it. Just consider the security detail, okay? We will obviously continue to have security provided for your events, but HOME is prepared to pay for a private guard to escort you whenever you leave your house."

The thought made Mr. DeVito's stomach twist into a pretzel. The last thing he wanted was a babysitter, but if his detractors had found a source of what amounted to murder in a bottle...did he really have a choice?

Stella sensed his unease, but did not choose to press the matter. "Just think about it. Now, be a good boy and go back to your office. Read the plan thoroughly. We've included what you should look for in this person, possible ways to convince them to go along with the plan if you don't manage to make them like you, and safe date ideas that will look good in the media.

"Study up so you're ready for next week. But don't feel overwhelmed. You need to be likable, not perfect. And don't worry. The event will be well-guarded, and every human will have had a rigorous background check."

"Yes, Ma'am." He tucked the folder under his elbow and stood to leave, fighting back the urge to tell his boss for the millionth time that he hadn't been a 'boy' for a very long time. There was no winning with her...

On his way back to his office, he stopped by accounting. Erin and Luna seemed hard at work, but looked up with smiles as he knocked on the doorframe.

"Oh, hey Mr. DeVito. What can we lowly accounting staff do for you today?" Erin asked.

The vampire chuckled and shook his head. "Lowly? Far from. But I need some budget forms for this week's soup kitchen and an acquisition form to send over to the hospital for the week. I managed to use my last copy of each last week without realizing it."

"Gotcha covered, Mr. DeVito!" Luna exclaimed as she spun her office chair and pulled open the filing cabinet behind her. "By the way, I heard that the apartment project has come to a bit of a standstill?"

He leaned against Erin's desk and let out a small sigh. "You heard correctly. I was there last week to consult with the contractors about vampire-friendly features, and nearly ended up with a brick between my eyes. It was pretty easy to dodge with my vampiric speed, but it's disappointing to see the citizens of city center being so violent over something as simple as apartment renovations."

Erin scowled. "Disappointing, but not surprising. Why do they feel threatened by tinted windows and self-closing garage doors? It's not like those are abnormal features even on human dwellings. It's ridiculous." The elf tapped her pen against the desk as her ears twitched. "Have you filled up every minute of your schedule with HOME projects again this week? You need to learn to take some time for yourself, if you ask me. Even *you* are sure to burn out if you keep throwing the candle in an incinerator."

"Yeah," Mr. DeVito replied. "But HOME changed my life, and I don't mind filling my schedule with changing the lives of others. Even if I don't end up being elected, at least I can keep handing out blood to vampires and shifter pills to werewolves to help prevent crimes of desperation."

CHAPTER 2

><><>**Amber**<><><

*C*rowds of admirers, constant proposals of marriage by
desperate, overweight, and frustrated housewives, and the
feeling that she had to constantly survey her surroundings to avoid
any unpleasant surprises were not things that Amber would have
listed when asked about her perfect life. Perhaps she should have at
least chosen a female pen name instead of Henry Allan Spencer...

Just two years ago, she had quite enjoyed her quiet life of creating
fictional romantic settings from the peace of her tiny apartment with
a cup of cocoa in her hand. The trouble had all begun when she made
the mistake of leaving the manuscript corner visible under her
mattress when her big sister Jade came to visit...

And from such an innocuous scenario rose the chaos that became
her new life. Jade refused to take no for an answer, and within months
the world was introduced to *Beneath Caribbean Skies*. Despite Amber's
complete lack of interest in romance in general, it seemed she had a
way of portraying it which sent her readership into a frenzy.

She supposed that she could be described as "loaded" at this point,
though all that had changed in her life was the replacement of her

ratty slippers and the acquisition of more expensive cocoa. The money was great, at first. But it took only a few months of unwanted fan mail to taint the ever-growing bank balance.

Her other unwanted acquisition in this whole mess was Gabriella. Gabriella was the nagging, persistent editor and agent she had been landed with. While Amber appreciated Gabriella's shark-like demeanor when dealing with the publishing company and advertisers for her...she was less thrilled about it when the shark turned on her.

Her latest campaign was Amber's second book...the one she hadn't planned on writing. "The market is sorely lacking in supernatural-related romance novels! The untapped potential is immeasurable! This is your opportunity to become *the* name in a genre!" Gabriella insisted. And because Amber had the hardest time saying no to the other women in her life, thus began *Finding the Blood Moon*.

Which, apparently, was the most pathetic piece of trash Gabriella had ever read, if the single yellow sticky note plastered to the front of the manuscript was to be believed. 'Uninspiring, bland, and illogical' she had called it, as if Amber was supposed to somehow magically know how human/supernatural relationships would play out.

Which was the incorrect thing to say, *apparently*. Next thing she knew, Gabriella was at Amber's door with a pages-long application, a pen, and a set jaw. "Fill it out and I'll deliver it myself," she demanded and handed Amber the paperwork before perching herself in Amber's favorite chair.

Amber balked when she realized this was a speed dating application, but Gabriella's eyes bored into her skull and seemed to physically rip her arguments right out of her brain. She squinted at the extra page of questions for supernaturals in disbelief. "Have you harmed or killed a human in the last five years? Have you ever been possessed? Is there a possibility that you have sexually-transmitted lycanthropy?"

Wow. They didn't pull any punches, did they?

But Gabriella made no move to lessen her glower. So, with a sigh, Amber had filled out the paperwork, including the background check release, without complaint. She returned it to Gabriella and several days later, showed up to the venue precisely five minutes earlier than was required.

She'd pulled out her favorite suit for the occasion: a brown number with a navy vest and bowtie. Despite her best efforts to tame her curly brown hair, it still stuck up every which way. Thin-rimmed, square-lensed glasses perched on her freckled nose. They gave her a bookish, youthful appearance quite fitting of her 25 years.

Perfect for a quiet author.

It felt strange to arrive by bus when the parking lot was filled with gleaming cars. It also felt strange to peek out the windows and see crowds of people with protest signs.

"Don't let the fae take our children!"

"Today our apartments, tomorrow our lives!"

"Fated mates are fake news!"

"Keep out crime! Keep out supernaturals!"

The protestors clogged up the sidewalks more and more thickly as the bus approached the venue. But the bus arrived without incident and, as a human, Amber had no issues passing the crowds. The venue itself had guards at the gate keeping the protestors at bay. Once Amber had passed the gates, their shouts faded and gave way to soft orchestral music.

The event was exclusive (and rather expensive.) Only those with acceptable answers on their applications were allowed in. In addition, the number of humans and supernaturals had been balanced. It had resulted in a bit of a lottery system for the humans, but Amber 'lucked out.'

She was sure the organizers had spent plenty of time attempting to make it less awkward, but there was only so much that could be done to jazz up a speed dating night. It was held in a large ballroom with methodically placed tables and high-brow decor. What might be considered 'romantic' mood lighting flickered between each pair of seats, and expensive bottles of wine sat on all four long tables.

Upon check in, the singles were given an adhesive name tag and a wine glass which would join them on their rotations. Amber noticed that humans were given red tags, like her own, while supernaturals received blue with an extra line for their species. Supernaturals were assigned a seat, while humans would rotate.

A small stage had been set up at the head of the room for the host. The center of the room sported a bar, a fondue fountain, and various snacks. Already the milling crowd filled the room and the hosts were busy getting the supernaturals settled in their assigned seats.

Amber watched them curiously, trying to see if she could tag their species before even meeting them. Elves were easy; their pointed ears and slim builds gave them away instantly. The palest ones were probably vampires, if she had to guess. But werewolves, witches, and shapeshifters? Without their blue tags, they might as well have just been humans.

Interesting. Even the elves aren't that different than anyone else. No wonder so many of the supernaturals that came out in the 60s already lived in regular society!

She overheard someone with a blue tag whispering to their companion as she stood in the check-in line. "Last year the supers changed seats. But the humans complained, feeling like we were stalking around the tables like tigers. I feel like these events are more catered toward humans than they are for us. It's almost insulting."

Amber almost found herself agreeing, but didn't have much time to dwell on it before the lights dimmed further to bring attention to the front stage. She took a deep breath and let it out slowly. *Here we go.*

"Welcome, everyone! Thank you to everyone who decided to participate in this evening's event." The hostess wore a lovely red dress and a fancy updo, braided and twirled with an inordinate amount of bobby pins and hairspray, no doubt. She was as garish as the projector displaying a slideshow on the screen behind her.

"You lovely singles have seven minutes to get to know each other before a bell will ring and the humans will rotate to the right. When you reach the end of the table, my dears, start back at the top! And most importantly, have fun!"

The hostess waved her hand and anyone who hadn't already been seated found the closest available spot at their preferred table. The options were 'female supernaturals seeking men,' 'male supernaturals seeking women,' 'female supernaturals seeking women,' and 'male supernaturals seeking men.' Amber took the seat at the top of the straight male supernatural table and jumped right in.

Despite her trepidations, the first few rounds weren't as terrible as she had expected. The handy tags removed the stress of asking people their names. And when she thought of this as a research event rather than an attempt to find a romantic partner, it became almost bearable. Already her little leather-bound notebook was filling up with observations and ideas, and a small smile was beginning to tug at the corners of her lips.

Again the bell rang and the human swapping commenced. Amber stood, thanked the werewolf she'd been speaking with, and slid to the next chair on her right. Her next date, Reuben DeVito, stood to greet her. He wore a light gray, 3-piece suit and vest combo with a lilac button-up and deep purple tie.

It was already too hot in the venue, so he had removed the jacket and hung it over the chair. His eyes drifted down to her nametag while his hand extended. "Amber? It's a pleasure to meet you. I'm Ben. Please, have a seat."

Amber scanned the vampire's sharp features and intense eyes as she accepted the firm handshake. The cold touch of his skin sent the tiniest of shivers down her spine, though she did a good job of hiding it.

"A pleasure to meet you as well, Ben." She settled into the chair and, realizing her eyes had latched to his teeth, dragged them away.

This was her chance! There had been surprisingly few vampires so far at the event, a real disappointment. Amber flipped open her little notebook, readied her pen in her left hand, and met Reuben's gaze. It struck her how contradictory those golden-flecked eyes were to the plastered smile on his face.

But there wasn't time for such things. Amber needed information for the novel, so she scanned her pre-written list of questions and jumped right in. "So, tell me a bit about yourself. What do you do for entertainment? If you could visit anywhere in the world, where would you go? What do you look for in a relationship?"

She looked up expectantly, her thin frame at full attention. Her soft, brown eyes were full of interest as she leaned forward and offered Reuben a smile, revealing an Amber that few people got to see. In her excitement, she didn't consider whether her question delivery was awkward (it was) or if she was coming across strong (she was). To her benefit, though, her innocent aura framed her like a child meeting an idol for the first time.

CHAPTER 3

><><>**Reuben**<><><

From the moment the event began, Reuben was having a terrible time. However, he did his best to keep it from showing on his face. He mentally went over the tips given by his PR team and hoped that his use of just 'Ben' would somehow throw people off the trail of recognizing him as 'Vampire Vito.' It was a slim chance and he knew it, but it would be nice to just be a regular citizen for one night.

What really bothered him was the nagging fear that any one of these people could be hiding a small vial of death in their pocket. Yes, they'd all had background checks. Yes, security guards stood around the perimeter of the room. Even a few extra guards were seated amongst the attendees undercover. But how long did it really take to inject a dose of lethal poison?

Reuben physically shook these thoughts from his mind. That was why he was here. Supernaturals needed security, and he was going to provide it. So he glued the media-beloved smile to his mouth and greeted each new human politely. And inevitably, they always began with:

"So, you're a vampire. Do you actually drink blood?"

He knew it was coming. The question came up in every conversation he ever had with a human. However, what they really wanted to know was if Reuben would drink *their* blood. He honestly should have gotten the answer tattooed on his forehead to save everyone some time.

But he instead stuck to the PR approved, scripted answer he'd always used. "Yes, I do drink blood and yes, it is human. HOME has set up ways for vampires to purchase soon-to-expire blood from blood banks, and the proceeds are then used to help fund human hospitals and treatments. There is also an option to register as a fatality blood donor when you register as an organ donor."

While it always seemed to give him a positive pass on the conversation, it never seemed to actually gain him any favor with the human across the table. The event was already starting to look like a complete failure. Human after human had taken a seat in the chair across from him, but he didn't feel any closer to finding a partner.

But then Amber appeared.

Reuben wasn't sure if he should be impressed by Amber's dedication, or worried that his name would be written in the woman's little death note. But what surprised him the most was the authenticity of the questions. He hadn't been in the dating pool for many, many years. However, he was fairly certain that these were the usual types of questions. They were the things that normal people looked for in a partner, rather than the curiosity of a human faced with a supernatural.

The second thing that surprised him was how enthusiastic the stranger seemed to be about meeting a vampire. He could see those chocolate eyes sparkling, which made him worry about something different…that this random woman was hoping to be turned. Despite it being thoroughly illegal to turn anyone these days, occasionally some nutjob thought being a vampire or werewolf sounded 'cool.'

The possibility kept Reuben's guard up, but he did his best to go with the flow. He mirrored Amber, putting his folded hands on the table and leaning forward. "I enjoy reading, binge watching TV, and hiking. Not that I have much time for hobbies…it's more like reading a few pages here, watching a few minutes there, and finding a quiet place like the bathroom to escape the chaos of my job for thirty seconds."

Reuben gave Amber a toothy grin and leaned back in his chair, allowing himself to feel more comfortable for a moment. "I would love to visit somewhere with penguins. Preferably Argentina or New Zealand, not Antarctica."

Amber began to laugh. "I don't think you'll find that many penguins in Argentina or New Zealand, but I suppose you could look!"

Reuben watched the woman's curls bounce as she laughed. He shook his head, finding himself thinking how pretty they looked. He even started feeling relaxed, which was...unexpected. "I suppose you're right. As for what I look for in a relationship, that's a bit of a doozy. But I would have to say I find intelligent conversation and honesty flattering."

He'd had no idea what would come out when he opened his mouth, but Reuben stuck the landing. If he was being honest, he *did* admire both of those in a friend, but he didn't have time for a partner right now. Work sucked his life dry already. He wouldn't be here if Stella hadn't made it *very* clear this was required for work and not just a suggestion.

Sensing it was his turn to ask questions, Reuben paused for a moment. He needed to know if Amber wanted to become a vampire, or had any reason to ruin the political career that he'd had fought so hard for. But unlike with the rest of the humans he'd spoken to tonight, he couldn't bring himself to ask such things directly.

So he set aside the pointed list of questions he'd memorized over the last week and went rogue. "What about you? What do you do for a living? Do you have a favorite place to wind down after a long day? And what is it you look for in a relationship?" Reuben asked the questions in the same rapid-fire manner, the corners of his lips twitching with amusement. "Oh, and what's your favorite candy?"

"I'm a bit of a writer, though not that great of one."

Reuben chuckled and waved a hand. "You know, you should give yourself some credit. I'm sure your writing is a lot better than you think." That *did* explain the extensive scribbling of notes, though. For a moment Reuben had worried Amber was a reporter with the amount of pages she had filled tonight, but the real answer put him more at ease.

A ruddiness appeared in Amber's ears. "It's kind of you to compliment my writing without reading it; thank you. Sometimes I think it's an author's curse to never feel like their novels are as good as others think they are. And the ones who do are writing absolute trash. But I suppose it was good enough that my agent requested I write a second, so there is that."

"I'm sure she's correct. Do you use your own name or a pen name? I'd love to look up your work, if you're okay with that. Or if not, that's fine, too!"

"Oh, uh. I use a pen name. But I don't like to let people link it to me," she explained, her hands waving in front of her as if warding off invisible attacks.

Reuben heard her heart speed up and he raised his own hand comfortingly. "Hey, that's understandable! That's why people use pen names, right? Sounds normal to me." Though it did make Reuben more curious what Amber wrote, if she didn't want to be linked with it.

"Yeah. For sure. As for winding down...well, my favorite places in the world are the public library and my little apartment. There's nothing like curling up in a quiet corner with a good book and some hot chocolate. Do you...drink hot chocolate? I must admit, I know far less about vampires than a human in the current climate should. But at the same time, I don't know what questions are polite and what questions are likely to result in me looking like an ignorant asshat. So I remain woefully uninformed."

Reuben lifted an open hand to again ease Amber back from her concerns. He'd had much worse, and Amber had provided the most fascinating conversation all night. "There's no need to apologize. It's not your fault! Information on vampires isn't readily available or widely taught. Yet."

He felt like he could ramble on and on about the amount of misinformation that terrified humans spread to cause more panic; however, this wasn't the time or place to rant. He did, however, make a mental note that Amber didn't know much about his kind. Perhaps she *wasn't* a crazed woman who wished to be sired after all. Yet another concern removed from the list!

Feeling better and better, Reuben settled back in his chair and stretched out one leg. "I used to enjoy a cup of hot chocolate after coming inside on cold winter days. I used to love how the mini marshmallows would melt into them... I'm not sure if that's a hot chocolate sin in your book, but I'll have to try it again now that my diet has changed."

"Marshmallows aren't a sin. No, not at all! I love almost any kind of hot cocoa variation. Marshmallows, peppermint sticks, caramel, peanut butter...almost anything. I learned how to make brownies out of hot cocoa mix one time! I was out of plain cocoa powder so I figured I could try using hot cocoa mix. It's basically just cocoa powder and sugar, right? It was awesome! And that opened up a whole world of mint brownies, pumpkin spice brownies, peanut butter cup brownies...You, uh...should try it some time."

A small smile inched its way onto Reuben's lips as Amber rambled. Despite the human's obvious nerves, it was enjoyable having someone converse with him as a fellow person. "That sounds lovely. Must be a fantastic way to use cocoa. Brownies are probably too much for my system, but I can imagine how good they probably taste."

"Ah, that's too bad." Amber offered a sheepish smile and glanced down for a moment to consider her answer to the third question. "In a relationship, I suppose I would look for similar things as you. Someone who can have an intelligent conversation rather than prattling on about inane politics and sports."

Reuben flinched at the mention of politics, but Amber didn't seem to notice. "And someone who can enjoy the quiet times would be nice too, without being too clingy. Not that I have much relationship experience to draw from...but I think those traits sound ideal. And my favorite candy is chocolate. The higher the quality, the better. I might be a little obsessed, if I'm being honest."

He noticed Amber's cheeks blush red yet again. Reuben couldn't tell whether he was the reason behind Amber's embarrassment, or if that was how she normally acted. For some reason, he hoped it was the latter.

Silence fell between the two for a moment, broken by Amber when she finally asked a vampire-related question. "So...when you became a vampire, did your interests or personality change much? I'm sorry if that's an awkward question."

Reuben reached over and placed his hand flat on the table, inches from Amber's hands and notebook. He was stunned that a human would ask him a deep question like that and gave a small, toothless smile. "Amber, rest assured, it's not awkward if it's a great question. Can I answer yes and no? After I turned, it felt like I needed to relearn how to be myself. My interests didn't necessarily change, but the rules for life had. It wasn't an easy transition back then, so the experiences may have hardened my skin a little.

"And it wasn't like I lost everything. I can't spend the whole day on a beach without getting third degree burns, but have you ever gone away from the city and looked up at the night sky? I had to find the beauty of life in other places... if that makes any sense."

Reuben regretted every word that came out of his mouth. It wasn't one of the usual questions with a repetitive answer. He wasn't used to letting anyone past his thick-crafted wall, or having to dig for an answer. What resulted was something more genuine than he'd expressed in a very long time. "Supernaturals like myself have to do the best we can with the world we're given, you know? We face struggles at every turn, but really? We want to be treated like everyone else."

"I see, I see. So if I had met you before, I'd generally be meeting the same person as now. This is all fascinating! I'm going to have to give Gabriella a lesson when I next speak to her. Unimaginative and unlikely my ass..."

Amber paused, seemingly lost in thought for a moment before returning to give Reuben context. "Sorry, Gabriella is my agent. She and I don't exactly see eye to eye on vampires. But I won't bother you with all that nonsense."

Despite his curiosity, Reuben kept his thoughts to himself for now. Slowly, he leaned forward and cupped a hand near his mouth. He didn't look intimidating in the least; in fact, it looked like he was about to share some juicy gossip and he wanted Amber to be included.

"You would have met the same me, yes," he whispered, "and you don't have to be so nervous. Just don't ask if I'll drink your blood or turn you, and I promise you won't look like an asshat." He smirked as he used Amber's own words against her in a playful way. He placed his hands back down on the table, and reached out to fidget with the stem on his wine glass.

"Is...that a thing that humans ask for? Fascinating! No offense intended, but I cannot imagine willingly joining the supernaturals while also knowing how they're treated. I know that humans can be...rude." She again reddened as her eyes focused on the movement of Reuben's fingers.

"It's not for the glamor," Reuben clarified. "It's more for the special abilities that we possess. Living forever has a certain ring to it. Though I am curious about one thing now, and you don't have to answer if it makes you uncomfortable..."

He looked up from his distraction, though his hand continued fiddling with the glass. "If you don't know much about vampires, are you here to meet a different type of supernatural? Pardon me if that sounds rude. I've met an overwhelming number of closed-minded people. It's not too often that I meet someone with such an open mind about *these* sorts of things."

Amber reached toward Reuben's hand out of reflex as the vampire's demeanor fell. She gripped his cold fingers and shook her head. "Oh no, no no. I came to learn more about vampires and what a relationship with one is like.

"At the risk of sounding like a creep...Gabriella told me that I needed to write a supernatural-themed novel next, but I didn't know enough about them, in her opinion. So she set me up to attend this thing. I wasn't here to pick up a partner. Just to gather information on vampires. I know it might sound kind of shallow, but vampires are my favorite supernatural group. I'm sorry!"

A breath caught in Reuben's throat while his eyes shot to their point of contact. The feeling of someone holding his hand for anything other than a formal handshake was...foreign. He couldn't remember the last time someone wasn't repulsed by his cold skin. But the warmth of Amber's hand felt like drinking a cup of hot cocoa on a winter day.

She seemed to realize then that she'd grabbed the vampire's hand and released her grip. Reuben didn't want to admit it to himself, but he wanted to reach out and follow the source of warmth. However, he stayed still other than blinking twice to clear his thoughts. "Uh, no need to apologize. That's a much better answer than I might have expected. Not creepy at all."

Less creepy than what I'm here to do.

Amber gave Reuben a soft, timid smile and continued. "I have enjoyed talking to you more than I ever expected I would enjoy anything about this event, so I-" She was cut off by the bell signaling that it was time to change partners again. The author sighed and closed her notebook without finishing the sentence.

On a whim, she flipped the book back open and scribbled something, tore out the page, and folded it in half before extending it to Reuben. "I...um, if you didn't find me totally weird and uncomfortable and you're not mad that I wasn't here to try to find a date, I'd love to talk to you some more. For research, you know." She placed the sheet on the table.

Reuben picked it up and slid it into his vest pocket for safekeeping. He swiftly stood up and gave a soft, respectful bow to Amber. "It was a pleasure to meet you, Amber. You've given me much to think about."

The human flushed and moved to the next person, though as the evening progressed, Reuben caught her glancing back at him whenever the person she was speaking with looked away.

CHAPTER 4

><><>**Reuben**<><><

The announcer picked up the mic and a slight squeal from it grabbed Reuben's attention. "Thank you all for coming tonight," the hostess said. "For the next hour, the tables will be moved apart and refreshments will be served. Feel free to wander the room and spend a little more time with anyone who caught your eye!

"If this is the end of our journey together, travel safely and we hope to see you again. If you're staying with us for the casual event, please be patient while we set up. Feel free to hit the restroom or get some fresh air while you wait."

Reuben slipped away quietly to take the offer on fresh air. He stepped outside to text his manager, grateful to finally be finished with the speed dating nonsense. After carefully examining his surroundings, he pulled out his phone.

REUBEN

Are you sure this will work?

STELLA

Shouldn't you be at the singles event, Mr.
DeVito?! If I find out you didn't go, they'll never
find your head!

Reuben sighed heavily, knowing how furiously Stella must have punched the text into her phone. He could hear her screaming the message in his ear and knew he had to reply, or she would call him right then and there. The last thing he wanted to deal with was speaking to her over the phone.

REUBEN

I am at the event right now. There is a small
intermission. Just taking a few minutes to
gather my thoughts.

STELLA

Good! Then go find yourself a decent human to
take home!

We need this plan to work out.

You know what is at stake.

But I know you're more than capable!

You have half the girls at the office hanging on
your every word. So make the magic happen
with a human. :)

And that was that. There was no arguing with the boss...so he better find someone to show off. Reuben took a deep breath of night air and stared up into the darkening sky. He *could* leave now and say the meeting was a bust. Everyone was either a creep or wanted something from him in a blackmailing sort of way, and he would have to try to find someone a different way...but that would be a lie.

There *was* Amber.

Not only did she make great conversation, but her story was something Reuben could work with. They both needed something out of this exhausting night. He reached into his pocket and extracted the slip of paper, smiling when it was exactly what he thought it had been: Amber's name and number in a barely legible scribble. He found himself oddly happy as he tucked the slip back into his pocket. Fine. He would do it.

Reuben wandered back into the hall with his suit jacket properly buttoned now that he wasn't sitting down. His hair had managed to hold itself together so far and his thirst was also at a minimum, so he figured this was 'best case scenario Reuben.' His eyes scanned the room of people; the crowd had thinned out a bit, but the majority of attendees stayed for the second portion of the event. The free food and wine probably helped…

Then he caught sight of the messy head of brown hair atop a brown suit wandering the crowd. Reuben subconsciously smoothed his jacket one more time before beginning his delve into the mass of people. He didn't get far before he was stopped by an eager woman gripping his elbow. It wasn't a polite grab like Amber had done with his fingers earlier; this was demanding attention. The woman was bouncing in her heels.

"Hey Ben, I wanted to speak to you a bit more! Do you have a second?"

It took everything in Reuben not to spin around and smack the woman's hand away. Once he calmed down from the adrenaline of suddenly being grabbed, Reuben instead gave her a big, toothy smile and shook his head. "I'm sorry, I'm looking for someone else." The woman melted back onto her heels and released Reuben's elbow, allowing him to continue his journey.

><><>**Amber**<><><

Amber considered leaving, but she knew Gabriella would be angry if she missed this second half of the opportunity she had given her. She was exhausted. Her brain and notebook were bursting with new information which she couldn't begin to sort yet. But with a sigh, she straightened her bowtie and glanced around the room to see who was staying. She found herself hoping that Ben would still be there, but she couldn't see him in the sea of people.

So she settled in an empty chair and pulled out her notebook, stalling in case any of the supernaturals she'd spoken with felt the desire to find her. As she skimmed the notes from her time with Ben, she kept having a recurring thought: The answers she'd been given to her questions were unexpected.

They were so...ordinary. Reading? Television? Simple hikes? She might as well have been speaking to any generic man on any generic dating app. It was simultaneously fascinating and a little frustrating. Obviously Gabriella had never sat down and spoken with a vampire! 'Unimaginative' her left big toe...She would be scanning her notes as soon as she got home and sending them to her agent in an email entitled "I'm Not As Much of a Lump of Cold Butter As You Seem To Think!"

Amber was also grateful that Reuben didn't appear likely to pry too deeply into her writing, and his calming gestures were...well, rather attractive, really. She took a deep breath and had to remind herself that she wasn't here to find a partner. She was here to do research.

But then again, was there anything wrong with at least checking out the options?

And so she stood and moved to the middle of the room. In the center of the crowd, Amber waited for anyone to approach her. She was surprised how affected she was that none of the other singles seemed at all interested in speaking with her further. The last seven years had been spent alone in her apartment, after all. But she was fairly pretty, she thought? Polite, knowledgeable? Not prone to fits of fancy or obnoxious jokes?

And yet here she was, standing alone in the center of a crowded room. She felt more unwanted than she had in a long time. Even Ben, who had appeared somewhat interested, looked to have vanished into thin air. "I guess I judged the interaction wrong," she muttered. She was about to head for the door and call the experience over when she felt a gentle tap on her shoulder.

"Excuse me. Amber?"

Amber turned back, startled, and found herself face to face with the handsome vampire. "Oh, hello Ben," she replied, feeling a smile creeping up where the frown had been only moments before. "What can I do for you?"

Reuben took a half step back and shoved both of his hands into his pockets, seeming a bit nervous. Amber couldn't help giggling to herself as she saw how flustered he looked. However, she waited patiently for him to gather his thoughts.

"I think I have an idea that might fix both of our problems," Reuben said finally, giving a reassuring smile before leaning toward Amber. The room was abuzz with music and chatter, making conversation from a distance difficult. "Would...you like to discuss my idea further somewhere a little quieter? We could go to a coffee shop, or I might be able to convince the librarian to stay a bit later if you wanted to stop by the library?"

Amber listened with growing interest, her heart beginning to pound in her ears. Was...was Reuben asking her out on a *date?* It was a little hard to tell; 'an idea to fix both our problems' didn't sound too date-ish, but coffee shops and libraries? Those were some of the most stereotypical date locations a romance author could think of.

The buzz of the surrounding conversation and music faded to nothing as Amber's brain filtered it out and focused solely on the person in front of her. This was a big step, no matter the intent behind the invitation. She'd been entirely a recluse since her book took off in fear of being discovered.

Then again, she had chosen a male pen name specifically to make it harder to link her face to her book. So perhaps it wasn't such a big deal after all? And so she did the bravest thing that she'd done since high school.

She decided to say yes.

"That would be delightful. There's a lovely little coffee shop a few blocks away that should be about empty at this hour? I...probably spend more time there than I should, if I'm being honest. But the owners are sweet and the place is open all hours. It's called Tres Leches and it's on Grand Street. I don't have a car, but it's not too far of a walk. Or we could get a taxi?"

It was at this point that Amber began to wonder if she was babbling and snapped her mouth shut like an iron trap. Her ears turned a little rosy and she fidgeted with the notebook in her pocket before working up the courage to say anything else.

Reuben took the opportunity to fill the empty space. "Oh, we can take my car, if you are okay with that. I live a fair distance from here, so I brought my own transportation."

Amber considered this option for a long moment; long enough, really, that it began to look like Reuben was worried she'd changed her mind. "I, uh…okay, that would probably be fine," she finally replied. "I did want to grab some of the food before I left, though, if you don't mind? I'm not one to pass up a free meal!"

"I don't mind, please go ahead." Reuben motioned to the small, but elegant food presentation the event had prepared.

CHAPTER 5

><><>**Amber**<><><

*A*mber slipped away to yes, get food, but more importantly to allow herself to settle down. Excitement and fear rushed through her veins in equal parts. It had been many, many years since a man had shown an interest, be it casual or more. In fact, the last had probably been her senior year of high school when Ryan had torn her life apart.

She shook away the thought, not wanting to cloud the possibilities of the night with the ghosts of the past.

The spread was simple, but she could feel herself beginning to salivate as she examined all of the (expensive-looking) confections. There were about a dozen varieties of chocolates and, after glancing around furtively, Amber put one of each on her plate. She then slunk away like a wild cat without bothering to grab any of the actual food.

For a moment she wondered if it was rude not to bring Reuben a plate. But not knowing what he could and could not eat made her feel like she was better off asking for forgiveness later.

While Amber busied herself at the buffet, Reuben waited patiently with his phone in hand, scrolling through a few emails to pass the time. She saw his eyes would flick up every few seconds to keep an eye on her. Was he trying to ensure she was coming back?

Though perhaps she was glancing at him just as frequently for the same reason. There was no use staying here if he was going to ditch her…The second the vampire made a run for it, so would she. In the opposite direction.

Only moments after disappearing, Amber returned to Reuben's side, half hiding her plate as if she feared judgment. Reuben *did* notice the large pile of chocolates, but chuckled to himself. Amber hadn't been lying about her love for them.

"I wasn't sure if you could eat anything they had on the table, so I hope you don't find it rude that I didn't make you a plate…" Amber's voice was full of feigned confidence, which clashed with her nervous body language. She hoped that if Reuben *did* notice she was nervous, he wouldn't automatically assume it was because Amber was afraid of him. On the contrary, she felt like she'd been given a golden opportunity to get information for her book.

"It's not rude at all, I promise. You don't have to worry about feeding me. Unless you see a bowl of hard candies like DumDum suckers. I might be a little disappointed if I didn't get a cherry flavored one." Reuben winked to show he was joking and slipped his phone into his pocket. "Shall we depart? Tres Leches on Grand Avenue? I think I know the spot. I'm ready to head out if you are."

Once Amber got over the shock of Reuben seeming unbothered by her awkwardness, she found herself relaxing. She nodded and followed him out into the night, sifting through her pile of chocolates to find the most appealing one to eat first.

The eyes of other attendees watching the pair leave prickled at the back of her neck, but Amber did her best to ignore them. Had she somehow managed to land the most desired man at the ball? Was…was she Cinderella right now?! Was that why everyone was staring?? The idea made her laugh internally as they left the crowd and entered the parking lot.

The parking lot was still decently full, but the protestors seemed to have disbanded after the sun went down. Amber was relieved, honestly; she didn't want to think about what might have happened if she and her new acquaintance had to pass through the gauntlet of angry people.

Reuben's eyes darted around the parking lot as he led Amber up to an all-black BMW Hybrid with tinted windows. The interior was also mostly black with silver trim. It, like its owner, was clean inside and out. Reuben reached into his pocket and clicked the key fob to unlock the doors, then opened the passenger door for Amber. "This is us. Please make yourself comfortable."

Amber's eyes widened when she saw the quality of Reuben's car. Okay, she was *definitely* Cinderella. Yes, Amber had more money than she needed for her simple lifestyle. But the pristine and costly vehicle told her that Reuben either made infinitely more, or knew how to spend it. She slid inside with care and ensured no crumbs of chocolate fell from the plate. It would be an absolute shame to ruin the cleanliness of her surroundings.

Reuben waited for Amber to be settled before he rounded the car and slipped into the driver's seat. She watched as he smoothed his hair and jacket, triple checked the mirrors, and turned the key. He looked even more nervous than she did, which actually made her a little more comfortable with the whole thing.

The car quietly started and the radio clicked on automatically to the local rock station. The volume wasn't loud by any means, but Reuben did turn it down a little nonetheless. He also typed Tres Leches onto the touch screen. "Looks like it's a short drive. You meant it when you said it was around the corner."

"Yeah, it's pretty conveniently located. I'm surprised it isn't more popular than it is." As she cautiously ate her pile of chocolates, Amber's eyes flitted around the cabin before settling on her ride companion. "Thanks for the lift. And for..." She paused for a moment, realizing that 'thinking I'm a little bit interesting' didn't sound great. "For taking time to hang out with someone as plain as me." There, that was good. Yes. Very social.

"Plain? Anything but! Almost every person I met today was an exact photo copy of the last *except* for you. They asked the same questions. They had the same reactions. They might as well have been drones. You've shown an interest in *me* rather than my vampirism and when you speak, I can tell your words are genuine. I haven't had that in a long time."

Amber fidgeted with her empty plate, struggling to let his compliments soak in. She didn't feel like treating Reuben like a person rather than a set of fangs was anything to be applauded. "It's hardly anything impressive, but thank you?" she replied.

They both fell silent, the sound of the engine keeping them both company the rest of the way. Reuben's driving was smooth, another victim of what looked like some sort of perfection filter. He slowed down for stop signs at the appropriate times and checked his mirrors regularly. His speedometer never extended 1MPH over the speed limit.

Before she knew it, they pulled up to a nice little establishment. It might have been described as a 'hole in the wall' kind of place, a red door set in brick with a window next to it smashed between two other businesses. Over the window was a small, striped-fabric awning which provided shade in the daytime to a single table and pair of chairs. The only indication this was a coffee shop was the stylized painting of a mug on the window and the shop's name in gold on the door.

Amber looked down to unfasten her seat belt. When she looked up, she was surprised to see that Reuben had arrived at her door in the flash of an eye. "Wow! So vampires *can* move super fast? Fascinating!!" She didn't know how that information might work into her novel yet. But she folded up her empty plate, tucked it under her arm, and pulled out her notebook to scribble herself a note.

For a moment she idly wondered if that same speed extended to other activities, but quickly shook the thought right out of her head.

She slid somewhat unsteadily out of the car and took a moment to regain her balance, chuckling as she did so. "Sorry, I'm a bit of a clumsy one." Reuben smiled and offered a hand, which Amber waved away. She could keep herself on her own two feet!

Reuben's manners thus far, though, had been impeccable and did their job: as awkward as Amber felt about going on this date, she found comfort in Reuben's polite manner.

CHAPTER 6

><><>**Amber**<><><

"*A*fter you, Amber."

Reuben held the door for Amber who hurried in and settled into her usual chair along the back wall, surrounded by the wonderful smells of coffee and baked goods. The cafe was fairly empty as she had predicted, for which she was grateful.

Reuben sat in the chair across from her and glanced around, also grateful for such little company. "You come here often, you said? It's nice. Smells great."

"Yeah, this is my favorite place to bring my laptop and write when I can't stand being in my apartment anymore. The change of scenery can help sometimes." Amber removed her coat and hung it on the back of her chair, settling into the familiar space before turning her bright eyes on her date. "That, and being able to watch people interact. That's a big help to making believable characters, you know."

Reuben nodded, cleared his throat, and scooted his chair closer. "How...how often do you watch the news or read about supernatural politics?" The nerves were obvious in the vampire's voice, though Amber was clueless as to what politics had to do with anything. Especially after she had specifically mentioned hating them at the event!

"I...can't really say that I pay too much attention to current affairs, I'm afraid," she replied. "The news makes me feel sad, so I don't generally watch it. I can get bits and pieces of what people are currently offended by when I scroll through social media, but that's about it."

A sigh of relief slipped past Reuben's lips. Before he could say anything further, the barista, Marissa, walked up to collect their order.

"Oh, Amber!" Marissa exclaimed, "Wonderful to see you again. And I see you have a friend!" She looked at Reuben and her smile faltered ever so slightly. "Oh, Mr. DeVito? Never thought I'd see you in a place like this." It was obvious from her expression that she belonged to the group who didn't look kindly on the face of supernatural citizenship.

Amber watched as Reuben physically flinched, ducking his head down when his last name was spoken. His eyes glanced around cautiously, though the few people in the cafe hadn't seemed to notice. The lack of movement in the shop let him relax a little bit into his chair. Amber's eyebrows lowered slightly, curious why her date suddenly acted so strange.

He clasped his hands together on the table in front of him and gave a toothless smile. "My apologies. I'm here with my new friend, Amber. Whatever she orders, please put it on my card." He slipped into his wallet and pulled out a silver credit card. "I'll have a raspberry tea for myself."

The barista did her best to hide the fact she was uncomfortable as she nodded and accepted the credit card.

A slight blush of secondhand embarrassment colored Amber's cheeks, which only deepened when her companion stole the check. Did that require they go on a second date so Amber could pay and make things equal? But would it be rude to ask for a second date purely based on that logic, even if Reuben didn't know that was the motive? Was she overthinking this entire thing?

Yes. Yes she was.

So to break the cycle of winding up, Amber cleared her throat and smiled at the barista. "One peppermint hot chocolate, please. With whipped cream and a hint of almond?"

"Your usual, then? To nobody's surprise," Marissa laughed, seeming more comfortable now that her attention had been pulled away from Reuben.

She hurried away and Amber pondered something about Reuben and the barista's exchange which had seemed...off. It took a moment, but the fuzzy thoughts of "Mr. DeVito" and "vampire" eventually melded into a coherent piece of information that she could examine.

Her eyebrows raised and Amber turned to face Reuben. "OH, you're *the* Mr. DeVito! The one everyone was screaming about on social media last week! I must say, opinions on my timeline were quite divided. But...I wouldn't have pegged you as single. Or interested in dating, if I'm being honest. But I must say, I'm glad to see that you're not the kind who flaunts his name around at events like we attended to ensure he gets the most attention. It's...refreshing."

"Oh, yes. Social media was on fire last week when they found out a new housing development would be built in the city, specifically having supernaturals in mind. Tinted windows, reinforced walls, doors and such." He looked down at the table and a wave of sadness lapped at Amber's gut. Reuben's face looked haunted, as if he could still hear the protest that had gathered outside city hall that day.

"I saw that one side believes giving supernaturals a place to live so close to the city center would increase the crime rate and put humans at risk. But the others say that supernaturals have been living in the area for years and not once has anyone taken a bite out of anyone's neck. I'm kind of somewhere near the latter, I think. A higher percentage of supernaturals doesn't necessarily mean a higher percentage of *problematic* supernaturals."

The barista returned at that moment with the drinks and placed Reuben's near the edge of the table. It could have been blamed on the angle she was handing the cups at, but the shaking in her fingers told a different tale. He gave a small, toothless smile and a head nod. A soft 'thank you' fell from his lips, trying not to scare the girl any further.

Amber's, on the other hand, Marissa placed directly in front of her while standing closer than was necessary. Almost as if she were using Amber as a shield, truth be told. "Was...there anything else I can get for you?" Both Amber and Reuben shook their heads and the girl scampered away.

Reuben sniffed his warm raspberry tea before sipping it; Amber supposed supernaturals could never be too cautious when it came to humans preparing their drinks. He must have found it poison-less, because he blew across the steaming surface and took a sip. "Mmm, that's nice."

It saddened Amber that her favorite barista would treat her new friend as if he were a ticking time bomb. She slowly stirred the almond cream into her cocoa with the peppermint stick, gathering her thoughts before returning to their previous conversation.

"I think...that people protesting the new housing complexes need to get over themselves. What they don't seem to realize is that these people who will be moving into those new apartments are already in the city living, working, and recreating. It's not like building a new complex is going to suddenly make new supernaturals appear out of thin air."

Reuben nodded, but Amber picked up that the protest wasn't something her new friend was excited to talk about, so she changed the topic. "So. You said you had a solution to both of our problems? I'm curious what kind of problem a high-roller such as yourself would have that you couldn't get someone to fix for you!"

She paused, seeming to consider her words. "Then again, I guess everyone has their problems, no matter what kind of life they are living. But I also guess I have to shut up before you can answer my question...sorry. I chatter when I'm nervous."

Reuben waved his hand. "Please, it's wonderful. You're the most real person I've met all night." He glanced around again, only continuing in a low voice when he saw Marissa had returned to the counter and no one else was looking in the pair's direction.

"Being the face of supernatural rights has its perks, I won't lie. I am able to help many supernaturals stuck in situations that I had found myself in years ago. They gave me a house, a company car, and I am invited to many dinner events...from the outside, it looks like I have the perfect life.

"But I am also HOME's token vampire that they get to drag around like a show dog. People outside the organization often get close to me for all the wrong reasons, which leads to me having an awful track record in the dating department. At least I get to enjoy a drink with a beautiful lady tonight."

Amber continued sipping her cocoa as she listened to Reuben, finding a bit of curiosity poking at the back of her mind. What situations had the man in front of her been in? Seeing how people today still treated vampires and werewolves and the like, she could only imagine how things had been before the Supernatural and Human Treaty.

The things he mentioned were so basic...a place to live, reliable transportation, the opportunity to interact normally with other members of the public. Had he struggled to maintain those base elements of a comfortable life?

But was a comfortable life worth basically becoming a pet of the public?

"I...I don't know what to say. I'm feeling embarrassed for my species. I'm sorry that people have treated you so poorly, but I hope that you don't let that get in the way of finding yourself someone that makes you happy. Because honestly? Happiness is the least that everyone deserves, in my opinion." She flushed at Reuben's shameless attempt to flirt with her, an experience that Amber didn't quite know how to respond to. When was the last time someone had called her beautiful?

"There is no need for apologies," Reuben insisted. "You have already treated me better than anyone else tonight, and by that I mean you treated me like a regular person. I used to be angry and bitter about my lot in life, but my views of the world have changed.

"I now understand people a lot more and have moved on from the grudges I used to hold on to so tightly. The world isn't as black and white as I was once led to believe. But also...If the world was filled with more people like you, it would be a wonderful place to live. I also wish the same happiness for you. But I wouldn't want anyone to be stuck with me for the rest of their lives if they didn't wish for it." Reuben's forehead crinkled. He reached up and rubbed it a few times with his palm, suddenly looking quite weary.

Amber shook her head and scraped at a bit of whipped cream stuck to the rim of her cup. "I mean, you've been so kind. I don't think that I would consider going out with you 'being stuck' at all. As long as the Ben I met tonight isn't all a facade and you're a mean, horrible person who turns upside down at the drop of a hat."

She chuckled, making it obvious that she was purely joking and didn't believe that to be the case at all. "I may not have gone to the dating event to find a partner, but...I'm glad you asked me out for drinks. I never would have thought that someone as important as you might be interested in a hermit author who can't bring herself to use her real name."

Reuben put down his tea. His mouth curled downward and he refused to meet Amber's gaze. She tilted her head, sensing the shift in mood. A frown was not the reaction she expected from her admission. Her stomach twisted into knots as she waited for Reuben to break the silence.

"I appreciate the compliments, but don't let the glamor fool you." Reuben continued staring at his tea cup and began swirling the last few drops of liquid, obviously stalling. Finally, he looked up and admitted, "The real reason we're here is because my bosses have twisted my arm into getting a public partner. They feel it would show that I am more human than everyone believes, and earn me a few extra points in the polls."

The warmth Amber had been feeling cooled and her breath caught in her throat as she realized what Reuben was saying. He...was being forced to find a partner? Did that mean that she was nothing more than the least annoying human he could find?

She suddenly felt less like she was on a date and more like she had been singled out for a job interview that she was unaware of. How silly of her to think that such a handsome and high-profile man as *the* Mr. Reuben DeVito would be interested in her!

But she did her best to keep her disappointment from showing on her face. She simply nodded while holding her cocoa cup in front of her lips. What right did she have to be upset, anyway? Reuben *had* prefaced this 'date' with the phrase 'to solve both our problems,' so she should have seen it as the business transaction that it was. And she'd already admitted that she hadn't gone looking for anything.

The reaction could have been worse...and so Reuben continued. "From the sounds of it, you need to know what it's like dating someone like me, and I need to date a human to be more likable. I know this might not be the most romantic way to put it, but would you be interested in pretending to date me?

"It could help both of us. I can give you accurate information on vampires, and all you would have to do is pretend to be my girlfriend until the elections. Attend a few publicity functions or events to be seen together. You don't have to actually talk to me outside prearranged 'dates' if you don't want to."

And there it was, as plain as day.

There was no way to convince herself she was misunderstanding. 'Would you pretend to date me.' Amber could see the benefits of such an arrangement. Gabriella would get off her back. Her novel would get more 'true to life' than she could have wished for.

But her Cinderella fantasy was crashing down around her. The clock struck midnight and the gift from the fairy godmother disappeared, leaving rags and a smashed pumpkin.

"There would be plenty of other supernaturals and humans present at all the events to study if you'd like," Reuben hurriedly continued, seeing the light fading from Amber's eyes. "And this may sound like a bribe, but they often have fancy desserts and food."

The last detail was one hundred percent a bribe. Who would sacrifice their safety for creme brûlée? Once his request came out in words, he had to know he sounded crazy. His eyes shifted down to his tea, ready for rejection.

A rejection which came on swift wings. It was entirely too much. Reuben may be a show pony, but Amber was *not*. With a bruised ego and a heavy heart, Amber found her head shaking. "N...no, I...I need to go. Thanks for the cocoa." Without another word, she pulled her jacket on and sprinted out of the coffee shop, leaving Reuben staring blankly at the empty wall in front of him.

CHAPTER 7

><><>Reuben<><><

*R*euben stared out the windshield of his car for a solid five minutes before he remembered something. His fingers entered his breast pocket and pulled out the slip of paper. At least he could make sure Amber had his number, in case she changed her mind?

After far too long spent squinting and guessing, Reuben typed the number into his phone followed by two emojis: a stack of books and a pen. It wasn't like he had another Amber in there; he simply loved adding emojis to everything. This did lead to him adding them where they didn't really belong, and also to his terrible choice of a first text.

A single bat emoji.

Sure, it might have been a clever attempt to cover up his botched proposal. Movies and legends had vampires changing into bats all the time, after all. But Reuben sure couldn't, nor could anyone he knew. He smacked his forehead, knowing he screwed up the moment he pressed send. So he sent two more messages. Back to back.

REUBEN

I'm sorry. It's Reuben.

Both of which were unnecessarily serious and well punctuated. Reuben tossed his phone into the passenger's seat with a sigh. Hell… he didn't even know how to *text* a woman properly.

Reuben exhaled a heavy breath. He knew this would be hard. He was wearing his heart on his sleeve and let Amber see the truth behind the curtain. This approach wasn't in the booklet that Stella had given him, but he couldn't bring himself to deceive Amber with a lie. He needed this kind human to know that he wasn't going into this wanting a relationship either.

He put the car in drive and began slowly making his way down the street toward his home. Out of habit, he scanned the road for any suspicious cars while the entire cafe scene played over and over in his head. How could he have done better? Amber had shown a level of interest in Reuben the *individual* that no one had shown in a long time. Every time her ears turned red or her thoughts began to tumble from her mouth, Reuben knew they were real.

He'd purposefully suggested suitable public places with a minimum number of people prone to gossip or violence. Neutral places where Amber would feel a bit more comfortable spending time with a vampire. It was imperative to the plan that she felt safe, rather than like she was caged in with a dangerous creature. But it was all for naught. He'd managed to scare her off by being too dang honest.

His hands gripped the steering wheel much harder than necessary. The look on her face when she realized he hadn't been actually asking her out lingered in his mind's eye and he shook his head in an attempt to remove it. "She told me she wasn't there for a relationship either, so why did she run out on me like that?"

Truthfully, he knew the answer. He probably would have run out as well if someone had asked *him* to be their trophy boyfriend.

By the time Reuben pulled up to his garage and parked the car, he was thoroughly disheartened. How was he going to win over the voters? It felt like an impossible mountain he needed to climb with no legs.

><><>Amber<><><

*A*mber didn't stop panicking until she was safe in the familiar surroundings of her dusty apartment. She lay in her underwear on the faded couch with her arm draped over her face. "I'm an idiot!" she whined for probably the seventy-fifth time, followed by a low groan.

Truly, she couldn't decide which action was more ridiculous: believing that Reuben had been asking her out on a date, or blasting out of the cafe and sprinting down the street as if being chased by a pack of angry chihuahuas intent on nipping her ankles. In a suit. A suit which lay on the floor in a heap as crumpled as her hopes.

Wallowing was one of Amber's most highly-refined skills and she could have lay there whining the entire night if she had not been so rudely interrupted by the dramatic opening bars of the *Jaws* theme. Her phone had been abandoned on the cluttered table by the front door. It flashed the heartbeat light of a pending notification that she had zero desire to read, even if she had noticed it before. But that theme meant only one thing.

Gabriella.

"I don't want to talk to you!" she yelled at her phone as she hauled her sulking mass off the couch and grabbed the offending device. "I'm not answering!!" she insisted…and then hit 'answer.'

"Hello?"

"You better have taken the event seriously tonight and asked all of those questions I sent you. I expect to see scans of your notes from the evening in my inbox tomorrow morning."

Right to the point, as usual. Amber stifled a sigh and attempted to keep her voice chipper. "Of course I did! And I will get them scanned before I go to bed. I've only been home long enough to catch my breath. Can't guarantee you'll be able to read them any better than the last batch you demanded, though."

"Your handwriting is a different problem altogether. But what do you mean, 'catch your breath'? Did you do something stupid again?"

"Depends on how you look at it, I suppose." Which was the incorrect answer, as the words were met with arctic silence from the other end of the phone. Amber could feel the wind chill through the speaker and shivered.

"Alright, alright. I went on what I thought was a date with one of the vampires from the event, and ended up running away when he asked me to go on further dates with him. I had misjudged the situation and I panicked."

"You RAN AWAY?!"

The screech assaulted Amber's eardrum painfully and she moved the phone away from her face to make the remaining inevitable assault more bearable.

"You managed to get yourself on a date, and then you RAN AWAY when handed the perfect opportunity for research on a silver platter?! You are lucky I'm already in for the night, or I would be getting in my car right now to come kick your butt myself!"

"It wasn't a real date, though! He wanted me to *pretend* to date him so he could look good to the public or whatever. And I am one hundred percent not okay with being paraded around in *public*, Gabriella! Where there are *people*. I would have to *mingle*. One night of that was more than enough, thank you very much." The expression of horror and disgust on Amber's face wrinkled her nose so hard that a small blackhead she hadn't noticed before began to sting.

But Gabriella wasn't taking any of her excuses. "He offered the silver platter with no strings attached? You seriously need to get over this homebound hermit phase and do the research. *Please* tell me you at least got this man's number so you can rectify this error? I am going to have to find another author to represent if you continue to struggle with producing a decent second book."

"No. No, I didn't."

Again her agent's voice began filling the air with the screeching of a banshee, but Amber had already stopped listening. This was going right back into the land of lectures she'd heard a thousand times already. She switched Gabriella to speaker and began clearing out the notifications on her phone, pausing when she saw a text from an unknown number.

Upon opening the thread, her heart skipped a little. The time-stamp told her that Reuben had sent the messages *after* the rejection, which surprised her. There was no way in a frozen-over Hell that *she* would have texted someone after such a rejection. "Okay, apparently I do have it. I forgot I gave him mine and he texted me."

The relief in Gabriella's voice was obvious. "Okay, good. This is salvageable! You text that man back and tell him you'd be *thrilled* to go along with his plan, or you'll be finding yourself a new agent. And you know that there are few agents as patient and understanding as myself. That would also mean revealing your pen name to another person."

Gabriella was playing hard ball tonight, and it was effective. The thought of having to switch agents was horrifying. Even if she decided not to write another book, having to deal with the advertising and whatnot of *Caribbean Skies* was not something Amber was willing to do by herself.

"Okay, okay. I will send him a message and see if he's still willing to proceed. Just...don't fire me. I need you!" Amber clenched her teeth in annoyance at the truth of the statement. She hung up to a chorus of 'you better' and 'don't forget the notes' and tossed the phone to the other side of the couch.

How, despite having zero interest in them, did Amber end up with such strong-willed women controlling her life? Wasn't that a married man issue?

><><>Mr. DeVito<><><

*A*mber wasn't the only one with woman problems. Mr. DeVito stood in front of Stella's office door and wiped his clammy palms on the inside of his pockets. He already knew what her reaction was going to be to his report, and despite holding out hope that his text from last night would get a response...his text thread with the author remained lonesome. The little bubble had changed from 'sent' to 'read,' but that was it. Which made Mr.

DeVito feel worse, because that meant Amber was deliberately ignoring him.

When he felt as if he had gathered enough courage, he knocked twice on the heavy oak door. His manager's voice granted him access and he stepped inside, making sure the closing door didn't slam before he stepped up and stood in front of the desk with his hands clasped behind his back.

Stella knew that trick and what it meant. She was the one who taught him how to hide his nervous hands, after all. "I'm going to hazard a guess that you were unsuccessful in selecting a human and convincing them to date you?"

"Your dang magic," Mr. DeVito grumbled under his breath.

Stella barely stopped herself from rolling her eyes; no matter how many times she insisted that she did not inherit any magic, that didn't stop him from accusing her of it every time her keen powers of observation caught him off guard.

A smirk flickered across Reuben's face for a moment. "You're not 100% right this time, though. I *did* manage to find someone, *and* I took her out for coffee."

"And then you messed it up, didn't you? Let me guess. You and your overdeveloped need to be overly honest told her that you weren't interested romantically and only needed her to pretend." Stella straightened a stack of papers on her desk while Mr. DeVito looked down at the floor like a scolded puppy.

"I thought as much. How hard would it have been to not be weird and treat it like you were *actually* interested? You were willing to take her out for coffee after a brief exchange at the event, so you might have ended up liking her for real after a few dates. Did you at least get her number? Or any backup numbers?"

As much as he didn't want to admit it, Stella had a point. Amber *was* pretty and interesting company, and the way she blushed and rambled at every little thing made her rather endearing. But he also had to admit that he was *not* in a place in his life where he was ready for a real relationship.

Mr. DeVito nodded, then shook his head. "I...got hers. But the rest of the humans showed little to no promise. The amount of times I shook a hand and felt them flinch was frankly insulting. If you didn't use magic, did you have someone following me? You are more scarily accurate at guessing the series of events than usual."

For the first time since Mr. DeVito entered the office, a bit of a smile and a chuckle broke through Stella's stony expression. "Mr. DeVito, I've known you for a decade and you are easier to read than the top line of an optometrist's chart. But all hope is not lost. I expected that it might take more than one attempt to find you a partner, so I had our research department compile a list of dating apps for you to download.

"I expect that you can find a suitable candidate in the next week or so. Let me reframe the plan for you. You will be the one pretending, and ask some humans on dates. Let it be real for them, and if you don't feel like keeping them around after the election, then you can send them on their way. It's only six months."

"Dating apps? Are you serious? How are you so cavalier about my dating life?"

Stella slid a single sheet of paper across the desk to Mr. DeVito and leaned back in her chair, again crossing one knee over the other. "Because it's not your *real* dating life. This is work. Think of it as politician practice. Tell the people what they want to hear. Make the right promises. All necessary skills for a successful political career.

"Obviously you don't want to register under 'Reuben DeVito' when you download those, or you'll attract all the wrong matches. Use your preferred nickname, and let me know as soon as you are successful. If you haven't found someone by next Friday, I will have the events department organize something to get you around more humans in person."

For a moment, Mr. DeVito was shocked at how callous Stella was about these humans and the public in general. He had gotten as far as he had on honesty and taking the title 'public servant' literally. The way his manager so casually told him to lie and sneak and play with emotions went against everything he stood for.

Yet...he shouldn't have been shocked. There were reasons that the elf in front of him had become the powerhouse behind HOME's curtain and kept it operating as long as she had.

Stella looked so pleased with herself, as if she was certain this plan was foolproof. Though that was because she would *make* the plan foolproof. If it took until Plan X, Y, or Z, she would ensure that supernaturals got their voice in law making, at least in this state. That was how Stella operated. She didn't see roadblocks; she saw inconveniences which would either get out of her way or be *pushed* out of her way.

"And have you thought any more about security? The dating event went smoothly, thankfully, but only because we had so many guards. How long are you going to be reckless?"

Mr. DeVito shook his head. Stella lowered her eyebrows, but with nothing more than a 'now be a good boy and get started on that' and a wave of Stella's hand, the vampire was off to his office to begin the next embarrassing chapter of the election saga.

Seated at his desk, Reuben took a moment to scan the list of apps and their descriptions, reading them out loud to the empty room. "Night or Eternity: generally used by more mature supernaturals looking for long term relationships. Moonlyte: Intended for short-term relationships or one-night rendezvous. Suckr: popular with the younger crowd. Ugh, these are *awful*." For around the sixty-third time in the last 24 hours, Mr. DeVito wondered if the election was worth the demeaning plan.

Then he remembered the feeling of starvation so strong it could crack the strongest moral code, and that was enough to prompt him to open the app store and begin Plan B. The last thing he needed was an even worse Plan C.

CHAPTER 8

><><>**Amber**<><><

*A*mber hadn't *lied*, exactly. She just...hadn't texted Reuben back *yet*.

She continued staring at the little bat emoji on the screen of her phone. It felt like hours passed as she willed her fingers to type any of the fifty-seven or so messages she had scripted last night as she lay in bed, unable to sleep. How hard was it to say "hey, I changed my mind and wondered if you'd meet me for coffee again" to a simple screen?

Or she could blame Gabriella. Now there was an idea.

With her eyebrows waggling, Amber typed out a message, deleted it, worded it differently, closed her eyes, and pressed send.

AMBER

Gabriella has changed my mind for me.
Coffee?

Too late to take it back now, she figured, and tossed the phone to the other end of the couch. She didn't want to see how fast Reuben did or did not reply, so for the next hour she showered, cleaned her room, made macaroni and cheese, and scrubbed her toilet. Only then was her fear of a bad response overcome by her fear of the unknown.

There was, indeed, a slowly flashing light on the top left corner of her screen, which filled her with a renewed sense of dread. Yet she opened it anyway.

> REUBEN
>
> Yes, absolutely yes. Tres Leches at 8:30 tonight?

Amber glanced at her watch and, seeing that it was still only two in the afternoon, sent back an affirmative. The next challenge became finding ways to waste the rest of the day until it was time to get on the bus. The answer *should* have been 'work on her manuscript.' After staring at it for a full thirty minutes and managing one sentence, however, she realized she was far too nervous to concentrate. Instead she hooked up her gamecube and played a solid four hours of *Super Monkey Ball.*

><><>Reuben<><><

*I*t was 8:25 when Reuben rolled up to the little parking lot. He shut off his engine and silently begged any deities that may be listening that this date would go better. The street was entirely empty and he didn't see Amber anywhere, but he waited until exactly 8:30 to open his car door and step out into the dim evening air.

It was tempting to linger outside the window and peek in to see if his date was already inside. Yet he knew better than to be a lurker. Nobody took well to a vampire loitering outside and peering through windows.

Luckily for him, he had barely made it up to the door when the bus arrived and expelled a ruffled Amber. She spotted the slender form of Reuben in the fading light and hurried over, sputtering excuses about late buses and pairs of obstinate grannies.

"You're only thirty seconds late," Reuben insisted with a toothless smile. "There is no need to be quite so flustered. I'm glad that you came at all. We can talk more about that when we're seated, however."

He held open the cafe door and followed Amber to the same table they'd occupied the night before. This time he looked much less out of place in a pair of well-fitted blue jeans and a pale yellow button-down polo.

Amber took a deep breath to calm herself as the same barista from the night before appeared at their table.

"Well, well, Amber. Two nights in a row?" Marissa teased with a grin. "Looks like things are getting pretty serious." She seemed somewhat more at ease tonight with Reuben, though she still remained on the human's side of the table. "What are we having tonight?"

"Same as usual," Amber replied, and Reuben again ordered his raspberry tea. No need to reinvent the wheel, after all. Once their steaming drinks had arrived and the pair had settled somewhat into the scenario, both stared at each other across their cups as if unsure who should start the conversation at hand.

Reuben leaned back from the table and cleared his throat. "So. I'm really glad to have heard back from you. You saved me from a week of scrolling through a dozen dating apps as a backup plan. I seriously owe you for that one."

The look of misery on Reuben's face was so unexpected that Amber began to giggle and immediately looked more at ease. "Okay, that sounds as bad as me having to find a new agent. Searching for a usable needle in a massive haystack, am I right? But it's Gabriella who saved you from that fate, so you don't owe me anything."

Amber hid her face behind her cocoa mug as much as possible in an attempt to mask how desperately she was attempting to look 'casual.' She was failing miserably, but Reuben gave no indication that he noticed. The last thing he needed was to screw this up again and have to go back to the abhorrent dating apps.

"I guess we better talk about the plan, then?" Amber said, her voice small and uncertain.

Reuben gave an affirmative nod and looped his finger through the teacup's handle. "Yes, that would be for the best. Let me see if I can explain the situation a little better this time…we only need to be seen in public a few times together, being affectionate enough to convince the paparazzi that we really are a couple.

"In exchange, you can enjoy all the fancy sweets at the dinners I'm forced to attend, while gathering information for your novel. And if you don't want to talk to me between events either, that's fine! I want this to be as low-stress for you as possible. And if you still feel nervous, I can have my boss assign you a security guard."

"I could probably make that scenario work," Amber replied, her eyes drifting toward the ceiling to avoid having to meet Reuben's gaze. Nothing in her face said that she was excited about the prospect, but Reuben was grateful she was at least considering it.

"It would be mutually beneficial, and I do like sweets," she continued, "but I'll have to warn you...I'm not super experienced with couple-type activity. I mean yes, I write about it. But it's not something I've had much experience in. I don't know if I can pretend well enough to pass the scrutiny of the public."

Reuben couldn't quite decipher Amber's true feelings about the whole situation and wished that he had Stella's magic. But Amber's lack of experience in the relationship department was...charming, somehow. Did Amber think *he* would be good at dating? Reuben leaned in and cupped his mouth as if sharing yet another dark secret. "Amber, I'll be honest with you. I have no idea what I'm doing either."

A soft laugh escaped his lips. It was quite sudden in the quiet cafe and he reflexively apologized. "I'm not laughing at you, I swear. I'm laughing at myself for being an absolute idiot. I guess I should have thought more thoroughly about this whole situation before attempting to drag someone into it. I might have been able to get Stella, my manager, to go with a different plan if I had enough backbone to stand up to her."

Amber joined Reuben's laughter. "No, no, it's fine! That means that we'll have to figure this out together. It also means that we don't have a whole lot of predispositions and ingrained expectations to get rid of before we can move forward. Fake or not..."

The pair fell silent as they sipped their drinks and ran circles of what they should say next. "I suppose," Amber murmured as she set down an empty cup and looked up at her date, "that you're going to want to discuss the details a little more thoroughly? How long the facade is to last? Where you want me to be and how close you want us to act? Do you want to...maybe...go on more quiet dates like this to practice?"

The last question caught Reuben off guard. It almost sounded like Amber *wanted* to spend time alone with him, which was ridiculous. Just yesterday she'd been so uncomfortable that she literally ran out. And today she was asking things like *that*?

Reuben nodded, rubbed his chin, and pursed his lips as he thought about Amber's less confusing questions first. "I'm not too sure about the exact length of time, but it could be up to six months. Which now that it's coming out of my mouth... sounds like a long time." He swallowed nervously. "Since I'm *very* rusty in the dating department, we could start slow and see what each of us are comfortable with."

"I don't think six months is that long. I've had ketchup sit in my fridge longer than that and it was still edible." Amber flashed Reuben a smile, only moments later seeming to realize how ridiculous that might have sounded. The tips of her ears turned bright red and she cleared her throat loudly. "But slow sounds good. I think...after a while, I could be okay with that."

Reuben chuckled a real chuckle, but chose not to comment on the analogy. "We could eventually tangle our daily schedules together if you wanted to go that far. Morning coffee, texting, shopping, and maybe spending the night at each other's homes if you are comfortable with that. We'd make it as real as possible while respecting each other's boundaries. Only if you want to! If you don't want any of that, that's fine. And it's only until the election! Then you are free to never talk to me again if you don't want to."

Reuben was giving such mixed signals and he knew it. Would they need to text each other constantly if they were only putting on a show for the public? Unless...he planned to expose their texting conversations by releasing screenshots to the media? But he also didn't feel like that would get him the kind of attention he needed. Perhaps he wanted to let Amber live out her novel material?

All the thinking and overthinking began to give Reuben a headache, so he gave himself permission to simplify and stop second-guessing everything. Hopefully Amber would understand how out of his depth he was.

"I mean, I'd be fine with texting each other at least. And going on a few dates. Between the politician who puts on a mask every day and the author whose job is to spin romantic fantasies, I'm sure we can come up with something convincing." Amber tapped the spoon on her empty mug and pushed it out of the way.

What was she actually thinking? Reuben opened his mouth to drill her about just that, but changed his mind. She was agreeing, and that was all he needed for now. It didn't have to be more complicated than that.

"That sounds lovely," he said instead. "We can both help each other out and maybe come out with a new friend." Reuben wasn't planning on tossing Amber to the side after their arrangement, but that would be up to her. He assumed most people would leave *him* after they juiced him dry of what they needed, based on his previous relationships.

In the meantime, though, perhaps it would be nice to have a friend. "Of course I'd be willing to spend alone time with you like this. I'd prefer it over crowded spaces any day of the week. A quiet corner in the library, a sunset hike, or lazing around the house all day in pajama pants. Everything would be more convincing if we got to know each other." He'd slipped his fingers around his teacup and nervously started to spin the remaining pink-tinted liquid in the bottom of the cup.

The smile that had disappeared yesterday returned. Amber reached out and wrapped her small, soft hand around Reuben's, stopping the tea swirling with a gentle smile. "I think all of that sounds *wonderful*," she insisted. "I'm not big on public speaking or public events, but it will be fine. We'll get you through the upcoming election, me through the second draft of this novel, and everything will be fine. And neither of us will have to attend any more dreadful speed-dating events."

"And I won't have to hope that I find someone as interesting as you on those awful dating apps," he sighed with relief.

There was still one topic they had to discuss, and while Reuben hadn't consciously left it for last, his subconscious almost certainly did it on purpose. "I do want to warn you about two other things.

"Because of my job, many events also have news coverage to generate hype around said events. And it's not just events, either. The paparazzi like to steal pictures whenever they happen to have a camera in hand. The cameras *will* snap a few shots of us.

"Hopefully we will have time to get comfortable first, and that a few pictures will be enough to keep my boss at bay, but it would look a little funny if we never spent any time together except at these events. People may become suspicious and we may have to purposefully spend some of our quiet dates in public spaces.

"The cameras might love me, but don't let my practiced smile trick you. The feeling isn't mutual. It's exhausting having to be perfect all the time. No one is perfect, I mean, but the paparazzi sharks circle until someone slips from the boat and hits the water. Then there's a feeding frenzy."

Amber seemingly hadn't considered the paparazzi on top of the public. Her face fell, though Reuben could see she did her best to appear brave. "I really hate paparazzi...As long as they don't trail us to my apartment. I don't think I'll mind a few candid photos, but you have to swear that they won't find out where I live. And also that if I have food in my teeth or a tag sticking out or toilet paper stuck to my shoe, that you'll tell me before it ends up all over the tabloids. And don't make me talk to people?"

Amber pulled her hand back with a nervous cough. "So yeah. We'll keep our employers happy and we can have some fun along the way. I'll do my best not to rock your boat." She gave Reuben the most genuine smile of the entire night.

Reuben blinked his stunned expression away, tucked his hands under the table, and shook his head twice. "Oh no no! I promise, no public speaking will be required. I wouldn't make you come to all of the boring press conferences, either. They are dreadfully dull and often run longer than intended. The galas, charity events and dinners that come with them is another story. And I hear you loud and clear about the address. I have no trouble keeping your home safe from nosy reporters."

Reuben's brow softened as his lips curled into a smile. Amber was kind of adorable, being so worried about such trivial things as tags and toilet paper. "I solemnly swear to keep a sharp eye out for a stray trail of toilet paper or catch you if you fall. It will be a team effort to paddle this boat. I have no intention of leaving you to drown.

"The other thing, though...It's not just paparazzi that I have to worry about. There are plenty of people who would resort to violence to keep me and other supernaturals out of society. I should be the one asking if you are okay being alone with me in the first place. I will, of course, try my hardest to be the best boyfriend I know how to be, and do everything I can to keep you safe. As long as you have no problem with boyfriends from romcoms and cheesy romance novels. They are...kind of the only examples I have to emulate." He shifted in his chair, suddenly looking a little shy. He wasn't knocking the genres; he was simply too embarrassed to admit that he regularly indulged in both.

CHAPTER 9

*R*euben really felt like he was approaching the finish line of sealing this deal. All that remained, really, was to ensure that Amber felt it was fair.

"Do you have any concerns about this arrangement? I could, of course, compensate you for your time. You're a writer. You must be busy with your own book signings and meet and greets on top of also writing a second book. I also realize this is a huge favor to ask of someone I've just met."

Reuben tilted his head back as he covered his eyes with one hand. Even he knew how crazy he sounded, begging for Amber to save him. A woman he met only 24 hours ago. "For heaven's sake, I must sound like a nut case."

"I wouldn't be paying you for the information," Amber insisted, "so I don't want you to pay me, either. I'm not an escort...but I think I'd be fine spending time with you. I let you take me to a quiet and deserted cafe on our first night of meeting, didn't I? For our situation, that might almost be considered a one night stand." Amber snickered, hiding her face behind her hand a little as she did so. Mostly to hide the growing blush in her face. "And how better to learn how to write a cheesy, romantic romcom-style novel than living one?"

"A one-night stand, huh? I hope it was as good for you as it was for me. Although, I hope this ends up being more than that. We could have so much more fun back at my house... with my own private library," Reuben shamelessly flirted with a quick wink. Now that the deal was practically done, he might as well start practicing.

Amber flushed more desperately at the flirting, but did take a few seconds to gather any remaining concerns she might have before answering Reuben's real question. "I don't have any big concerns. But...I've never done a public signing. I...kind of use a pen name, remember? And try not to connect *this me* with *that me* in public, you know? Maybe someday, but I..."

She paused, struggling to come up with a phrase that didn't make her sound like the absolute antisocial hermit that she was. "You already know I am afraid of the public life you lead. So maybe this will be good for me. Spending a little time in the light while not having it right on me, I mean. I think I sound like the bigger nutcase, here." Amber awkwardly rubbed the back of her head.

This caught Reuben off guard and made him more curious about what kind of books Amber published. Were they too embarrassing to link to her real face? Or...were they so poorly received that she didn't have any fans to do signings for?

"Don't be too hard on yourself. I don't blame you for wanting to hide your true identity. People can be vicious animals when they want something. As much as you've made me curious, I won't connect you with, or ask you to tell me, your pen name in any way, if that is what you wish."

The kind words relaxed Amber somewhat. She still had one important question, though. "I appreciate that. I also have to ask, do you mind if I end up using some of our experiences in the novel? I know that sometimes people get uncomfortable with that, so I try my best not to use real-life experiences in my writing. But I think in this case, some of them might end up woven in."

She paused for a moment, searching Reuben's face. "I can let you read the manuscript before I send it to Gabriella, if you'd like. Kind of like an alpha reader, so you can ask for anything you want to be removed."

Reuben thought about the writer's question for a moment. If she wanted to use their experiences, was she actually writing a romance novel? She hadn't told him what genre she wrote, he realized, and the idea of being *in* one of his romance novels brought a smile to his face.

Sure, their dates and experiences could be used, if that were the case. But then he thought about all the political details that could be used against him. "I just realized that I didn't actually ask what kind of book you're writing. I'm guessing it's a romance, from that question?"

"Oh, yes! Sorry, I didn't realize I hadn't told you. It's a vampire and human romance story, though I have no idea where it's going yet."

So he *was* right! Since she was a romance author, had he perhaps read her work and didn't know it? That would be funny. Maybe someday he would find out.

For now, he replied, "I don't see why you couldn't use our experiences together. However, I wish to keep the details of my job a secret. There aren't many vampires with positions like mine and the trail would eventually lead back to me."

It was risky, he supposed, but Reuben smiled and nodded while saying, "Can we agree to keep my name and specifics of my job out of it?" The fact that Amber was willing to let him read the manuscript was promising, and would provide a great way to see what kind of writer his fake girlfriend really was. What with her pen name being off limits, and all.

"And of course I would love to read it. I appreciate you giving me permission to remove things that I don't feel comfortable with. As long as it's not made up tabloid nonsense about vampires and you write about true experiences, good or bad, I don't think I will have a problem with it. This will be a good way to give humans and vampires a look into what an actual friendship would be like between our species."

"OH," Amber sputtered, "the vampire in the book would have a different occupation and lifestyle than yourself. I figured that some of our dates and things might end up as details in the plot line, that's all."

"Just dates and scenarios? I don't think we'll have an issue, then." If

Amber thought some of their interactions were interesting enough to sell to the public, then she could write as much as she pleased. It would be interesting to see the human side of an interspecies relationship, too. It might help him in the future.

The clock on the wall began to chime 10pm and Amber looked at her watch with a gasp. "I'm so sorry, I've kept you out so late! I hope you don't have anywhere to be early in the morning? I tend to be a night owl, but I realize not everyone keeps a writer's schedule. Maybe...we could plan a second real date sometime soon? Even though we're pretending...I had a fun evening. And I'd love to see you again." Amber's face began burning at her overly honest and forward admission.

Reuben was surprised how fast time flew by when he was spending time with Amber. It was...easy. He waved his hand with a smile, unbothered. "Oh, don't worry about it. I'm a night owl as well. Long periods of sunlight exposure isn't healthy for my skin."

He finished the last of his tea, long since cold, and pulled a crisp twenty dollar bill from his wallet. The barista may not have been as welcoming toward his kind as Amber, but she hadn't thrown him out or attempted to poison him either time he'd visited. He appreciated that amount of kindness, at least, and set the bill on the table.

"I would love a second date," Reuben said after standing and pushing in his chair. "I thought tonight was going to be a train wreck like yesterday, but you have been the highlight of my month. You are an absolute delight." He gave a huge smile and held out his hand for a handshake out of habit. It would have been awkward if he took his hand back now...but he also wasn't ready for a goodbye hug, either. He needed to work on the mental side of this whole thing before he was ready for such an affectionate gesture.

"I do my best to be a positive experience when I do interact with others," Amber replied and grabbed her coat from the back of the chair. The extended hand put a look of surprise on her face, but Amber took it and gave two solid pumps, the standard and non-awkward handshake. Moderately firm grip, not too long or short...Reuben could see in her eyes that she thought way too much about such things.

Reuben glanced at his car through the window, then to Amber. "I would offer to give you a ride home, but I feel it would be easier to keep your address a secret if I just make sure you get on the bus safely. It feels weird, but under the circumstances..." It felt wrong leaving Amber to fend for herself entirely, and he wanted to ensure she made it home safely. Grown woman or not.

"Hm? Oh, uh, yes. That would probably be the best idea. I wouldn't want to bother you with driving me home, anyway. Though with the riots going on lately, I have avoided going out at night when I don't have to. So waiting with you would be great. Also I'm rambling again, I apologize."

There it was again, that awkwardness that he'd already figured out marked her nervousness. Reuben couldn't help being amused by it as she slid her coat over her arms and buttoned it for warmth.

When she was ready, Amber looked up and gave Reuben a wink. "I had a good time, too. It was nice spending time with an attractive man such as yourself two nights in a row."

Reuben grinned at the cheeky compliment. He was about to come back with a witty remark when Amber leaned against a chair in what was intended to be a 'cool' pose, only to misjudge how much weight the chair would handle at that angle and have it begin to tip over. She stumbled and Reuben's lightning fast reflexes shot his hand out. His fingers wrapped around Amber's bicep, ready to hold her up if he had to.

Amber, however, managed to catch herself after a minorly dramatic stumble. "Well, that was close," she laughed, more out of embarrassment than actual amusement. "I almost fell for you already, there."

"Oh, um. I'm sorry. Are you-" Reuben mumbled, fearing the invasion of personal space wasn't permitted. However, the cheesy pickup line caused him to laugh. "Smooth, Amber. I'll have to dust off my pickup lines."

Reuben waited with Amber for the bus to arrive and watched it pull away before slipping into his own car. *Wow. That did go a lot better than I expected,* he thought as he sat in the parking lot, until his phone vibrated.

AMBER

I'm glad that not-a-bat Reuben didn't 'lose' my number the moment we parted yesterday. I look forward to our next 'date.'

CHAPTER 10

><><>Amber<><><

*A*mber's face and heart were warm as the bus pulled away. Not only had she been on her first on-purpose date in a very long time, but that she had the promise of a second in the near future as well! Even if it was…well, fake.

The word 'fake' tasted bad on her tongue, but she did her best to convince herself that this would be beneficial. A trial run, one might say. Practice for when something real came about. A business venture.

Amber did feel quite inadequate, if she were to tell the truth. She was about to thrust herself out of her quiet, peaceful life of cocoa and writing, and into the public eye. Would she be convincing enough? Would Reuben ever see her as more than a pawn in his election?

Did she *want* that?

But if she did end up dating a public figure, would people start digging into her background and find the link between her and Henry Allen Spencer? A curious mob was as intimidating as an angry mob, and the last thing she wanted was to be outed.

Yet the grin on her face was wide and ridiculous, and Amber couldn't find it in herself to care. She was too wrapped up in the night and everything that had come from it. She couldn't help feeling like she was living within one of the romcom storylines that danced constantly through her head.

What kind of story didn't have a little turbulence, after all? There was certainly a lot to think about tonight while she fought with her insomnia. As she lay in bed, she started wondering how this was really going to work out. Maybe...it would be nice. And tomorrow the real work began.

And work it was. She spent the next two days staring at the computer screen. Amber repeatedly pulled up the old manuscript, remembered Gabriella's blunt response, and closed it. No, there was no saving that piece of garbage. She would have to start over.

But after a few pages, she'd again repeat the cycle. Anxiety settled in and she continuously deleted entire passages. She was unsure if she had gathered enough information yet to come up with a believable story line without passing into offensive stereotypes and assumptions.

Around 9pm on the second day, she found herself slamming her face into the keyboard and checking her phone every hour. She needed more information from Reuben, but hadn't gotten any messages since her little attempt at a joke. Had she been offensive and Reuben ghosted? It was quite possible. Maybe she should text him again? No, that might come off as needy...

Why did real life socializing have to be so difficult?

By the third evening, Amber was convinced that she'd screwed everything up. No texts, no calls. Only radio silence. She stared at the new first chapter of *Finding the Blood Moon* and sighed heavily. "How am I ever supposed to finish this crap knowing that I already failed at interspecies romance? I might as well throw in the towel and find a new career. I'm not cut out for this field!"

She was solidly staring at the trash can icon when the faint buzzing of her phone caught her attention. The screen was lit up with "NOT A BAT MAN" as the name of the caller, and Amber nearly knocked her chair over rushing to grab the phone. Her finger lingered over the answer button, suddenly struck by a case of the nerves. But she managed to work up the courage to press it and answered in a voice far calmer than she expected, "Hello? Yes, this is Amber."

><<>Mr. DeVito<><><

*E*xactly four days had passed since Mr. DeVito attended the singles' event. His PR team had been circling like a pack of hungry wolves looking for good news and gossip. The vampire, however, seemed to be keeping the information to a minimum. All they had gleaned through their intensive stalking was that the event had been terrible, but their rep had managed to find a decent girl. They had coffee twice and that was it. End of story.

And it wasn't just the PR department who were sticking their nose into it. Rumors of Mr. DeVito's current stunt had spread through the office like wildfire, despite every person who heard the tale being sworn to secrecy.

It became apparent, however, that he hadn't *done* anything else with this mystery woman when everyone realized he had nothing more to say. That, and the fact he was in the office almost 18 hours a day. That was not going to make the plan successful.

So, ever the one with another scheme between her ears, Stella purchased a set of aquarium tickets. If the first date didn't satisfy their gossip needs, then maybe a cute second one would.

Mr. DeVito had barely stepped into the office when he was beset by his manager. She had an uncharacteristic smile on her face and Reuben was instantly on his guard. "I know that look. What do you want today, Boss?"

Stella feigned offense and shook her head at the rep. "What do I want? I don't want anything. I have something for you." She produced a small envelope and handed it over, watching attentively as he opened it and scanned the tickets inside. "Those are for friends and family. You know, to reward you for working so hard these last few months. The campaign trail has been extra difficult this year, what with the uprisings and protests. We figured somewhere beautiful like the aquarium would give you a place to relax."

"Not to mention it's super romantic," piped up Luna. "The low lights with silent fish slowly swimming their way around their tanks, jellyfish bloop bloop blooping without a care in the world! I'd love it if a cute man would take *me* to the aquarium."

One of the interns interjected with, "I prefer a picnic in the park, myself!" while another began prattling on about playing in the rain and camping under the stars. The conversation got everyone distracted enough that Reuben was able to sneak away to his private office. There he slipped the tickets into his pocket and turned on his computer to begin once again chipping away at the mountain that was *work*.

By the time Reuben pulled into his garage that evening and closed the door behind him, he was spent. He wanted nothing more than to drop onto his couch and stare at the television blankly for a while. He placed his keys on the little shelf by the door and pulled off his suit coat to hang it on the rack. As he did so, the little envelope from earlier fell to the floor.

Reuben picked up the tickets and fanned them apart between his fingertips. Cute little stingrays were swimming in the background, with a group of people enjoying the view. A deep breath entered his lungs and he pulled out his phone. He held it, screen off, for way too long as he debated on inviting Amber. Would she think this was a romantic date? Or was it...too childish?

Then again, he knew why he was being given the tickets by Stella. It was very much a thinly-veiled demand which he would be wise to follow. And he wasn't doing this for himself, after all. Thousands of supernaturals were relying on him to give them a voice. If he failed now, the likelihood of a supernatural legislator being elected in the near future dropped to almost nothing. At least, that was what he'd been told.

Though he had his own reasons. When he turned in 1986, he'd lost his family, his possessions, his career, and his life as he knew it. And there was no way he was going to risk losing HOME and starting all over again.

Reuben's thumb tapped 'call' on Amber's name and he took a deep breath. With each passing ring, he became more worried that his girl-friend wouldn't answer. He'd almost given up when he heard a voice on the other end of the line. "Hello?"

"Hello, Amber?" Reuben asked, a little too formally. He hadn't been home long enough to shed his politician mask. "I was wondering if you were interested in fish. No! I mean yes, but not just fish. They have sting rays, sharks, tide pools…" He didn't consider that he'd started to list various attractions he remembered seeing during one of his visits to an aquarium as a child.

Only half-way through did he realize he was attempting to convince Amber this was a fabulous idea without telling her the reason behind the list of sea creatures. It finally struck him that *he* was the one rambling on about nonsense without asking a question this time. He ran a stressed hand through his hair. *He needed to focus.* "I'm sorry. What I meant to ask was, would you be willing to go to the aquarium with me? I have this extra ticket…"

Reuben sighed as he paced his kitchen. He should have texted. Three dots at the bottom of his screen were preferable to the awkward silence that would undoubtedly follow the vampire's insane memory of the aquarium.

"Um, yes, I do like fish," she stammered, all semblance of cool, calm, and collected disappearing from her tone. "In tanks. And in the actual water I guess, but they're easier to see when they are in tanks. I mean, yes, the aquarium is cool. And I'd love to go. With you, with you. Not just go. But with you. Like you asked. Sorry, I'm awkward. Yes. I would love to go to the aquarium with you. When did you have in mind?"

Reuben had placed his back against the wall and tilted his head upwards as he waited for a hard *no* after his utter failure. However, Amber. Wonderful Amber. A huge grin spread across Reuben's face, teeth and all, knowing that the author was feeling a similar way.

"No, no. Not awkward at all. It's charming," he reassured as he rubbed the back of his neck with a free hand. What he wanted to say was 'adorable,' but he wasn't sure he could get away with calling her that. "How about next week? We could meet outside the aquarium at 8AM next Thursday? I'm pretty sure I can get my manager to block out that morning for this. I know we're not early birds, but it shouldn't be too busy when they open. "

Meaning if the place was crowded and one visitor caught wind that Vampire Vito was down there with them…he could already see half the crowd swarming him while the other half dragged their kids in the opposite direction. Cameras would forget the fish and turn on the couple faster than he could blink. Zero out of ten experience all around. "And I hope you won't be disappointed, but I'll try to dress down for it. Make it less conspicuous for a greater chance at a peaceful date."

"8am sounds alright. Just means I have to go to bed early. And don't worry, it's not your suit that I agreed to date. Even though it did look quite fine. Oh well, baby steps I suppose. I'll be sure to wear something inconspicuous as well. I'm looking forward to seeing you again."

Relief flooded Reuben's non-working veins that the time and date were favorable. If the wait had to be longer, the anxiety working up to it would kill him. Again. At least he had work to distract him between now and then.

Scenes and scenarios from warm, cute movies began running through his head, replacing any thoughts of cursing Stella for her win. "Perfect. 8AM Thursday it is. I'm looking forward to our aquarium date, too. See you then!"

><><>Amber<><><

*A*mber found sleep to be rarer to come by than usual for the next week, even with the sleeping medication. Equal parts excitement and nerves ate away at Amber's consciousness until she slowly began drifting away each night.

She wasn't quite sure why she was allowing herself to get so invested in this whole relationship thing, but what could she do? Getting overly wrapped up in the details was *such* an author thing to do.

The alarm broke through Amber's troubled dreams Thursday morning and pulled her into reality. Remembering why she actually had an alarm today, the author launched herself out of bed and into a fast shower.

Amber began digging through her closet as soon as she exited the shower, shivering and still slightly damp. What did someone wear to a casual second date? How casual was "casual"? Soon a pile of considered and discarded clothing options covered her bed, and Amber had wandered into the areas of her closet that had been undisturbed for half a decade. Jeans were the obvious choice for pants, but... She frowned in frustration until her eyes fell on a ridiculous camouflage-print polo that her sister had purchased for her once upon a time. She *did* say she'd wear something inconspicuous...

She shaved, applied her favorite perfume, and put on her outfit. She looked a little bit like a military mom in her jeans and camo shirt, but shrugged and put her wallet and keys in her pocket. The taxi she ordered arrived moments later and she found herself standing outside the aquarium at five before eight. It was a beautiful morning; only the lightest and fluffiest clouds dotted the azure sky, and the air had already begun to warm.

Not seeing Reuben right away, Amber sat down on a bench near the entrance and pulled out her phone. She opened the Google docs app and pulled up her most recent draft. It was still only about twenty pages long and not leading anywhere in particular, but at least she didn't want to delete it anymore. She began focusing on the vampire's first interaction with the human love interest to pass the time.

><><>Reuben<><><

*R*euben rose with the sun, giving him plenty of time to get ready for the date. And ample time for getting distracted. Despite having few casual clothes, deciding what would be appropriate for a public date proved to be a challenge. He dug through all his long sleeved shirts, figuring he would try to cover as much of his pale skin as possible. Dark clothing would make him look more sickly, so the lighter the outfit, the better.

Eventually he stood in front of the mirror in a pale-tangerine, long sleeved shirt. The top two buttons of three remained undone to reveal a plain white tee beneath. For pants he had selected a pair of gray, slim-fit jeans and a plain black belt. A backwards ball cap, white sneakers, and black aviator sunglasses completed the look.

It was perfect.

He drove himself to the aquarium and felt like he was doing quite well on time, until he couldn't find the entrance to the parking garage. The center of town was a mess of construction cones, detour signs, and groups of pedestrians pedestrian-ing where they should not be.

By the time he pulled into a parking spot, he was decidedly running late. His innate need to be perfect was screaming at his mistake and he flung the car into park when he found a space. Yet he still took a few extra moments to scan his surroundings, paranoia prickling the back of his skull.

The extra shade provided by the concrete structure was a godsend; the day had dawned as brightly as possible with little to no cloud cover. Of course. Reuben slipped on his sunglasses, otherwise unable to withstand the level of sunshine. He walked around to the front of the building, his eyes scanning each person he saw. Yes, he was still technically two minutes early. But it would have been his standard ten if parking hadn't been an absolute nightmare.

Reuben spotted the woman he was looking for, sitting alone near the entrance of the building. She hadn't stood him up! Gratitude filled him to the brim and he paused in the shade of a tree to watch her for a moment. Even in her ridiculous outfit, somewhere deep in his brain echoed the word 'beautiful.'

He couldn't keep the grin from his face as he strolled up and spoke. "I hope you weren't waiting long. Here, let's get inside real quick..." He grabbed the handle of the door and opened it, letting Amber enter first, but following swiftly behind.

The vampire's sudden appearance startled Amber; Reuben could hear her heart begin to race, though it quickly calmed when she turned and saw who had spoken. "Oh, no, a few minutes is all," she replied with a cheery grin.

Her eyes lingered on his face; she seemed interested to see that the small exposure to the sun left a soft, pink blush on Reuben's cheeks and nose. At least, that was his assumption for why she was staring. He tried to hide his face, but it was too late.

For a human, it would have been considered a healthy glow. For vampires? It was a reminder that Reuben really should have put on sunblock. He watched as Amber pulled out her little brown notebook and scribbled a note for later.

Inside and away from the windows, Reuben removed his sunglasses and got a real look at his date. "You almost would have blended in if that shirt didn't look so great on you," he teased, giving Amber a shoulder squeeze and a charming smile while looping his sunglasses away on his shirt collar.

Amber's own cheeks flushed at the compliment and she waved her hand vaguely. "Oh, you know. Just have to look half as good as my other half, while keeping my own brand of humor at the same time."

The first order of business was to trade their tickets for full-day wristbands. "Would you like me to put those on for you, dear?" the desk attendant asked.

Reuben shook his head with a smile that said 'I've got it, thanks.' One touch of his clammy skin would give away his 'I'm a normal human' ruse. As he walked away from the desk, he began (poorly) attempting to put the wristband on himself. He tried to use his thigh to hold it, leaning over and fumbling with the flimsy piece of paper until he sufficiently looked like an idiot.

Only then did he give in and look up at Amber, a bit embarrassed that he'd declined the employee's help only to ask for Amber's. With soft puppy dog eyes he mumbled, "I'm sorry...would you mind helping me? I can't get the sticker off..."

The friendly ticket lady applied Amber's wristband with practiced ease, then Amber turned and watched Reuben struggle. Her eyes glittered with amusement. "Of course, sweetheart," she replied.

Reuben's eyes had been concentrated on the wristband, but swiftly shot up to Amber's face when he heard the word 'sweetheart.' If he had still possessed a beating heart, it surely would have skipped.

CHAPTER 11

><><>Amber<><><

As she fastened the wristband, Amber giggled at the look on Reuben's face and found her hands lingering on his a little longer than necessary. It felt...different than when she had reached out instinctually to calm her friend. Her author brain railed against the cliche of 'stomach butterflies,' but in this moment, she couldn't think of a more fitting description.

Suddenly she began wondering about the proper timing of affectionate gestures. Was a second date too early to attempt holding hands? Had she already committed a faux pas with the pet name? And in a relationship like this...who took charge of those kinds of advances? In an attempt to break herself of the spiral of questions, Amber shook her head and looked at the double doors which led into the aquarium proper. "I, uh. Guess we should go in then, hm?"

The first room of the aquarium flickered in waves of blue and green, the only lights coming from within the floor-to-ceiling tanks adorning three walls where schools of tropical fish flitted back and forth. Water-filled pillars in the center of the room extended to the ceiling while jellyfish floated peacefully in their blue-lit water.

The silence of the room rested like feathers on Amber's ears and beckoned her in to enjoy its peace, while the cool air tugged her arm hairs upward.

Amber attempted to hide her excitement as she went from tank to tank, staring at the fish and reminding herself not to press her forehead to the glass and leave smudges. "I did a little research on the aquarium last night, because I've never been to this one," she said, her voice instinctively low in the quiet room. "Apparently it's set up like a gradual spiral, each room deeper underground than the last."

"I've never been here either, despite living here for an entire decade." For the most part, Reuben followed Amber from tank to tank, figuring that that was the couple thing to do. He liked the tropical fish; they were cool.

However, Reuben *loved* the jellyfish. His eyes followed one from the middle of the column all the way to the top, where the soft current turned it around in a lazy arc to continue its cycle back down. By the time he looked up, Amber was standing in the doorway into the next room.

This one was much brighter and louder with a jungle theme, vines hanging from the fake trees that extended high into the air. Rather than fish, the displays contained land creatures such as boas, birds, and various lizards. Birdsong filled the air with cheerful colors.

Amber paused in front of an enclosure containing moderately-sized crocodiles and stared at them in wonder. "I sure wouldn't want to meet one of those suckers outside a cage," she murmured, turning back to look at Reuben. "Look at how big their teeth are!"

Reuben gave Amber a long stare. "Sure, their teeth might be long, but I would hardly call these guys suckers," he remarked, tapping Amber on the shoulder with his fist.

It hadn't occurred to Amber that her usual slang might not have been the wisest choice of words in this company. "Oh, crap," she cried, slapping her forehead. "I'm so sorry...I didn't mean anything by that. I'll remember to use a different descriptor!"

The vampire's solemn expression cracked into a soft grin. "It's fine. Now you know." Reuben patted the shoulder he'd rapped and moved along to the tank of red-bellied piranhas, then pointed to the little fish without touching the glass. "Now these guys? They are so cool. Look at their glittery bellies!"

Amber hung her head and followed Reuben over to the piranhas, crouching down to examine their belly scales. Reuben dropped to a knee next to her, his shoulder brushing hers as they stared into the tank.

Amber felt her chest tighten as if someone had placed a belt around it and squeezed. Her heart beat a little faster and her pupils dilated. She cleared her throat and attempted to reply normally, "They are much prettier than all the cartoons would have you believe. And much calmer."

Amber managed to keep her voice calm, but Reuben could sense the biological response. He backed up a little bit and his fingers began to twitch, so he hid them in his pockets. He continued on the path with his hands stuffed to the bottom of his pockets where he picked at the lint.

But Amber didn't notice the shift in mood. She simply followed Reuben, meandering down the sloping trail which curved around the other side of the snake cages and opened up into a large, well-lit room with a shallow pool in the center. Within the twelve inches or so of water were starfish, stingrays, and other touchable critters.

Her face erupted into pure joy as she sat on the stone edge of the water, peering down where the rays flapped and the horseshoe crabs slowly crawled along the sand. She reached out and stroked the smooth top of a ray as it swam by, fascinated by the texture of its skin. It felt...a little like Reuben might if he was wet, she supposed. Not at all slimy. More cold and rather soft.

Since it was early in the morning and the creatures hadn't spent all day being poked and prodded by small hands, they were quite active and willing to swim up to her before flitting away.

Amber ran her finger across a few starfish and was interested to discover that they also didn't feel anything like she'd expected. From the dried ones she sometimes found in beach-side gift shops, she would have thought they were rough, like sharks. However, they were quite squishy and her finger glided over their skin with little friction.

Reuben stood in the entryway of the room, watching as Amber

played with the aquatic creatures. He couldn't seem to tear his gaze away from the dazzling smile that crinkled the corners of Amber's eyes and pulled one side of her mouth up farther than the other.

Her unbridled joy was infectious. "Come on! Come play with me!" she called, and when she waved Reuben to her side, the vampire's bad mood evaporated like liquid nitrogen in the sun.

Reuben took a breath of Amber's excitement and walked up to the pool, pushed his long sleeves up, and plunged his arm into the cold water. Each creature that zoomed by was fair game and his fingers explored their forms with great interest as he walked along the edge of the pool. Yet he was extra careful with them, not knowing how fragile they were.

From her vantage point sitting on the floor, Amber watched Reuben interact with the exhibit. He *was* handsome. And he hadn't appeared to care when called a pet name before. Perhaps...she could continue using them, then?

If nothing else, perhaps it might net her another one of those wide-eyed looks that she'd gotten the first time. It had made her heart race to be looked at that way and she couldn't help wanting it again. There still weren't any other people in the room, so she allowed herself to be brave for a moment.

"Hey babe, you look pretty hot from this angle when you lean over to play with the stingrays," she called from across the pool, accentuating it with a wink. She felt stupid right after, but dang if it didn't feel good to openly flirt after so many years of being single. Even if it was in an empty room and with someone who was only pretending to be her boyfriend...Be that as it may, she followed her flirtatious comment with a wolf whistle.

Reuben's focus was yanked away from the sea creatures. Suddenly, Amber felt like she was the most interesting thing in the room and had Reuben's undivided attention. "If I'm giving too much time to the rays and not enough to you, let me know, darling. I'll be right over," he teased.

The response came out of the back forty and Amber couldn't breathe. Rogue butterflies had gotten stuck in her throat, that was it.

Instead of replying, she attempted to hide her blush and ran to another pool in the room which contained small sharks.

Signs all over this tank read "DO NOT PUT HANDS IN THE WATER," but also had a small dispenser to the side which, when a quarter was inserted, would dispense some food that could be tossed in.

Amber fished a little change from her pocket and when she sprinkled the pellets over the water, the sharks began snapping them up. She began to laugh, somehow enchanted by how excited they were about the food. Perhaps because it reminded her of someone. That someone being herself.

Reuben followed Amber to the next exhibit, but remained a few feet away. Amber closed the gap and gave him a little handful of fish food. "Feeding time!" she exclaimed, waiting expectantly for her date to toss it in the water. She couldn't help but find herself looking Reuben up and down, liking the casual style as much as she'd liked the suit. As far as arrangements like theirs went, she could have a worse partner.

He tossed his food near Amber's and the sharks gobbled up the new pellets, their little fins slapping the surface of the water and splashing in their excitement. "These are quite fun. But there is no amount of money you could pay me to get in a little cage surrounded by full-grown sharks," he said with a shiver.

"We'll see about that," Amber replied, giggling at Reuben's sudden nerves.

CHAPTER 12

><><>**Amber**<><><

Satisfied with their interactive experience, the odd pair walked toward a cave framed in the carcass of a sunken ship. Darkness gave way to towering walls of water held back by floor-to-ceiling glass. And not just walls; the ceiling and center of the floor were also transparent.

Monstrous, silent forms swam past the glass, their scaly forms sleek in the azure water. Sun shone through the water, casting shifting patterns of light on every surface. The reality of Reuben's earlier joke set in. They were *definitely* in a glass cage surrounded by huge sharks.

The breath caught in Amber's throat as she stepped into the jaws of the cave. Looking out across the room, she watched Reuben as he hugged the wall, avoiding the unique experience of the see-through portions of the floor. For a moment she wasn't sure if she'd be able to walk out into the room at all. But Reuben appeared quite capable, so Amber took a deep breath and stepped inside.

She followed Reuben around the edges of the room to the front where she could see the entire tank laid out before her. Her eyes were riveted by the muscular beasts and the way they moved so effortlessly through the water. Movement near the top of the tank also caught her attention and she pointed up excitedly. "Look! There are turtles in there too!"

Reuben looked over to his date and closed the few steps of distance between them to see where Amber was pointing. At first her shoulder grazing Reuben's was their only point of contact as the pair stood watching the sharks swim by, but then Amber had a crazy idea. Maybe it was the mood lighting, the lack of an interactive exhibit, or the fact that Reuben gave her a warm feeling on the inside, she really didn't know.

But Amber reached out, touching her date's forearm, and gently trailed her fingers down his soft skin until her fingertips touched the vampire's smooth palm. Intentionally, for the first time. She carefully and slowly laced the pair's fingers together and gave a soft squeeze.

Amber didn't back down from her brave act, testing to see how long Reuben could tolerate her purposeful touch. Her heart began racing as if it wished to leave her chest and her blood rushed to opposite ends of her body, making her hands and feet feel hot.

For a split second Reuben froze, but he softened as Amber's fingers interlaced with his own. "You know, I haven't met many like you that would willingly accept me like... this."

Reuben's voice was low despite being alone in the enormous shark tank. He stubbornly stayed facing the exhibit, avoiding looking at Amber. "But I'm glad that I get to share these new experiences with someone who is unbelievably kind and as welcoming as you are."

"I..." Amber muttered, not sure how to respond to such kind words. "You don't give yourself enough credit. You are far more than what equates to a medical condition with no cure. Even after your life so drastically changed, you have chosen to help others. I think that is more impressive than a socially awkward author who isn't brave enough to put her own name on her writing."

Reuben pulled his hand away suddenly and left Amber looking bewildered. He pretended to be distracted by the biggest shark in the tank swimming over them and pointed with the hand he'd stolen back. "Oh wow. Look at that!"

Had she done something wrong? Amber pulled in a deep,

steadying breath and nodded. "Wow, that thing is massive! Is it a great white?"

Maybe it was the adrenaline talking, or maybe Amber needed to get herself out of the awkward situation. Whatever the reason was, she managed to gather the courage to walk to the open glass floor in the center of the room and watch the sharks drift by right below her feet. There was something intoxicating about knowing how much sheer power surrounded her on all sides. Power and danger – like the man she had chosen to spend time with.

Logically, she knew she should be afraid. Terrified, even. Yes, she was nervous, but she wasn't *afraid*. Something drew her in rather than pushing her away and, for once in her life, she wanted to run toward the danger.

And so, she did. As warm waves of confidence lapped at her, a smile spread across her face and she returned to the window where Reuben stood. She slipped her hand into the vampire's and turned toward the tunnel which led to the escalator.

"Shall we keep going?"

><><>**Reuben**<><><

*T*he tunnel was made of a half-tube of glass with coral on three sides. More tropical fish swam from one bit of coral to the next; clownfish and blue tangs flitted around in flashes of bright colors. Amber settled on a bench halfway down the tunnel and patted the seat next to her. "Why don't we take a little time to enjoy the ambiance? Unless you've got places to be. I don't have anything going on today other than attempting to write, so I've got all the time in the world."

"I'd like that." Reuben took the offered seat and pulled out his phone to see if he had any emergency notifications. Nothing appeared but a handful of work emails that he could read later. Granted, he didn't have any cell service down here, but surely that had nothing to do with it! "Seems like they can manage without me for a few hours. Besides, I'd much rather be here."

"Good!" Amber replied, reaching out and grabbing Reuben's hand again. "Then I'll keep you to myself as long as possible!"

Reuben's eyes finally turned to her, wanting a second glance at the person who made his 'Top 3 most exciting things of year' list. He was caught off guard yet again by Amber's insistence toward romantic gestures, but chose not to pull his hand away again. Her warmth soaked into his finger joints and traveled up his arm toward his still heart. The ice there began to sweat, creating grooves in the smooth surface and weakening his resolve one fraction of a millimeter at a time.

As much as Reuben believed and tried to convince everyone that he wasn't a terrible monster, hearing it from Amber's mouth still made him feel like a fraud. It could have been that his expectations were set way too low for the general population, but he expected the other shoe to drop at any moment. For Amber to pull back her hand, laugh that summer sunshine laugh of hers, and break the spell.

Yet Amber was so close. Their arms were touching. Their fingers were still linked together. This could have been one of the most romantic dates Reuben had ever been on, but he wasn't here for romance.

Yes, Stella had told him to let things be real for his chosen human if he needed to, but for him…this had to be business. Just the thought of getting too close to Amber and making her think there was more filled him with a sense of guilt.

He was saved from his dark thoughts by a soft splash announcing the arrival of a diver who was delivering the day's breakfast to the fish. They all rushed toward him and he began spreading pellets, which the tropical creatures devoured cheerfully.

Amber smiled and watched the man as he swam around cleaning the glass and display items, and playing with the fish as they swam through his fingers. "That looks like such a fun job," she sighed, jumping as a massive sea turtle swam over the pair.

Reuben nodded silently and watched the fish for a few moments. Between the well-lit area and the diver who had hopped into the water, he felt a little more control of his thoughts. Any awkward feelings he had toward their arrangement he filed away under a 'need to revisit later' category. "Was becoming a writer your dream job? Or are you considering a change of occupation after seeing the diver?"

As much as this was an arranged and decidedly staged relationship, it didn't have to be an empty one. Reuben wanted to get to know who he was spending his free time with and it would make their relationship look more real in the long run.

Amber considered the question for a moment before answering. She shook her head with a sad smile. "No, I never intended to write for a living. Writing romance novels was something I enjoyed doing in my spare time, and I once made the mistake of showing my older sister. She's the one who insisted other people might enjoy reading them as well...and I guess she was right.

"That's not to say I am not grateful to be doing something I enjoy, but sometimes I wonder if there were better options. I don't think I'm brave enough to be a diver, though!" She chuckled and ran her thumb over Reuben's knuckles.

The more Reuben learned about how Amber's writing career began, the more he was intrigued. However, he also began to realize how introverted she really was. Which wasn't a bad thing, but public events might be an issue if too many people gathered. He would have to keep an eye out to make sure Amber didn't become too uncomfortable. "I'm glad you enjoy it, even if it wasn't your first choice. And I don't think I could be a diver, either."

"So what do *you* enjoy when you're not working? I mean, we touched on it a little bit the other day, but I'd love to hear more about you. What does the daily life of a vampiric politician look like? I'm sure it's much more interesting than the life of a socially-anxious writer." Amber looked directly into Reuben's eyes, that same interested glitter he'd seen at the speed dating event shining in them.

Reuben rubbed the back of his neck, once again feeling like the most boring person on the planet. "I guess I can do a lot of fun things at night without having to worry about the same precautions as everyone else. Rock climbing without gear. Hiking on paths less traveled. Swimming deeper without needing to breathe. As far as my day to day life goes, I'm a bit of a workaholic. But I do like music, reading and hiking."

"Those sound so adventurous," Amber replied, leaning a little closer to Reuben.

"Oh, and I collect some movie memorabilia," Reuben continued, "my favorite being a few battle-ready lightsabers, if you're a Star Wars fan. A guilty pleasure purchase that I may have spent a bit too much on." He had never once gotten a chance to use them with anyone. He was sure his politician buddies would judge him into the ground if they found out he had hobbies deemed childish, and the public didn't need to know.

The mention of Star Wars made Amber's face light up. "I don't think that sounds boring at all! I can't say I'm much of an outdoor-swoman, but I am a self-proclaimed nerd. Star Wars is awesome! Though I'm a pretty casual fan. Just a few posters and knickknacks. And shirts. And socks. I really, really love fun socks. Jade thinks they're ridiculous, but eh. It's not like anyone other than me sees them, most of the time."

As if for emphasis, Amber lifted her pant leg to reveal tall socks with pancakes on them. "I have a stupid collection of them, but the thing is, socks are useful and don't take up a ton of space."

Reuben was feeling more than a little lost as Amber reclined against him, despite laughing at the sock reveal. As great as the date had been thus far, Reuben couldn't decide if Amber had feelings for him, or was simply playing her part beautifully. After all, pretending to be his girlfriend was what Reuben had asked her to do. But this all felt so *real.*

Maybe he needed to take this for what it was worth, thank the heavens he found someone so willing to play the part, and enjoy the ride. After all, what crazy human would have feelings for a vampire?

Reuben finally chuckled and leaned back against the bench, his eyes following the diver. "You know...it's so peaceful with the fish and the water and the plants swaying in the current. I can't believe I haven't been here before. I'll have to come back soon. Maybe they do memberships? That would be put to good use. Probably won't be as peaceful when all the kids start showing up, though."

As if summoned by his words, an entire class of second graders came pouring into the shark tank. The volume in the little tunnel went from a 2 to a 10 instantly, filled with the sound of running feet and excited squeals.

Though Amber was fine with children, the noise was a little too much for her. Her hands went instinctively to her ears and she scrunched her eyes closed. This only lasted a moment before she flushed and shoved her hands in her pockets. "I think it's time to go. We can rummage through the gift shop and see if they have anything fun?"

Reuben's eyes squinted at the children with distaste before looking at Amber. He was already starting to stand up when his date suggested they leave. "Yes, please."

CHAPTER 13

><><>**Reuben**<><><

*N*ow that the seal had been broken, Reuben figured he was safe to reach for Amber's hand to lead her toward the escalator. There was something...empowering about openly acknowledging his relationship, real or not.

Amber accepted Reuben's hand and followed him to the escalators. She stepped onto the moving stairs, wobbling a little as her feet were swept away faster than the rest of her.

Reuben steadied her by placing a gentle hand on her lower back. "Oh, careful there."

The escalator emptied into the gift shop, as expected. A soft hum thrummed in her throat, her happiness finding its own way out without her noticing. Her eyes scanned the variety of brightly colored, aquatic themed merchandise.

"Hey, Reuben, what is your favorite animal? On land, I think I'd say mine are wolves. Underwater, stingrays." She wandered over to a display of various plush creatures and ran her hands over the fluffy fabric. "Mmmm, soft," she murmured, a smile crossing her face.

Reuben couldn't help but notice the little pep that Amber had in her step. He again followed his date around for the most part, not interested in the overpriced, logo-covered items, but enjoying watching the other person. "My favorite animal? Land is penguins. I love how fluffy the emperor babies are. For sea creatures, it would have to be the octopus. They're highly intelligent and I love how they can change colors."

Stepping up to the plushie shelf, Reuben stroked a very soft stingray. With a mischievous grin, he picked it up and moved it up and down so the wings would flap like they did in the water. He flapped over to Amber and gave his date's head a soft bop with the plush before setting it down on the shelf and walking away like nothing had happened. Amber stared with widened eyes while Reuben strolled away as if he hadn't done something ridiculous and adorable.

He stopped at a spinning display which held little keychains with various names on them. He turned the display, frowning at the 'A' section. 'Amber' seemed to be sold out. "How do you feel about nicknames? Like Gem? You know, since amber is a gemstone?" Reuben had to admit, he found it kind of adorable.

"I'm okay with nicknames. Whatever you want to call me is fine, as long as it's not 'late to dinner.'" Amber chuckled a little at her own dumb joke and began scanning the mugs, thermoses, and tumblers. "How do you feel about Benji?"

The same shelf had caught Reuben's attention as well; he walked over, his eyes scanning each glass. They did have a stingray mug that Amber could use for her hot cocoa. "Benji, huh? Well, it's definitely not something the public would expect. I like it."

Reuben smiled and continued browsing, feeling an odd warmth in the pit of his stomach. "Would you like something? A stuffed animal or a mug? I might pick up an octopus thermos for myself." At least it would be useful; Reuben used thermoses to keep his breakfast blood warm.

Normally he used a solid color to keep up his perfect vampire politician persona; the public probably wouldn't take kindly to a 'Come to the Dark Side' thermos filled with blood. But maybe a cutesy octopus supporting the local aquarium would be fine? At least it would be easy to keep track of, ensuring his human coworkers didn't get a mouthful of Joe instead of their cup of joe.

Amber looked at the mugs, spotting a purple one with a little spotted stingray. She picked it up and examined it for a few moments before nodding. "This one is pretty cute. I think I'll get it so I can remember our first real fake date." She turned a particularly cheesy grin in Reuben's direction. "I think, so far, that it has been a particularly successful one. At least, from what I have gathered empirically through studying other relationships."

Once the pair had purchased their finds, Amber grabbed Reuben's hand and placed a little item in his palm with a grin. "There. This way you can subtly proclaim that you are taken. Or at least you can show the paparazzi parasites something to convince them. I guess it depends on if you want to qualify yourself as taken or not..." Amber's voice faded away and, yet again, her ears reddened. "I...I think I would. Even though it's for show, I feel like it counts."

When presented with the little object, Reuben was deeply confused. He looked down to find a keychain of a baby penguin with "Gem" emblazoned across the bottom.

It had been a long time since he had received a meaningful gift. Most 'gifts' were from his office, handed out to everyone, and were mostly pens, logo-covered mugs, and other useless merchandise that cluttered his office.

He blinked at the little penguin a few times in shock before responding, "Thank you. I will use it right away." Reuben slipped the keychain onto the set of keys that were devoid of anything fun, smiling at how embarrassed Amber got from handing it over. "It might be for show, but I appreciate the thought nonetheless. I am happy to be claimed by such a wonderful woman."

><><>**Amber**<><><

*A*mber grabbed Reuben's hand and half-dragged him toward the parking lot, mostly to keep people from seeing her blush. She found herself wishing that they didn't have to part ways so soon, but her mind was spinning emptily on ways to keep Reuben at her side a little longer. They'd already done coffee...but maybe she could swing a movie? He *had* said that his work could do without him for a few hours.

It had been so long since she'd had a friend she could ask to do things with that Amber wasn't sure how this whole thing worked. She was also surprised how comfortable she felt with Reuben after spending a grand total of a few hours together. Even when this whole relationship farce was finished, she found herself hoping they could remain friends.

And so, Amber took a deep breath and did something brave, yet again. That was seemingly becoming a pattern these days. "Hey, if you don't have to hurry back to work...do you want to maybe catch a movie? I don't know what is playing, but I'm not feeling like I want to go home yet. I'm having way too much fun."

But Reuben was too distracted to answer. By the sun. With his one free-ish hand holding the gift shop bag, he lifted it up, grabbed his sunglasses, popped them open in one smooth move, and slipped them on with another. He tried his hardest to walk at Amber's pace; however, the sun had risen higher in the sky, giving off stronger midday rays. Even with his sunglasses on, he squinted and tensed up slightly.

His hand gripped a little bit tighter on Amber's, like a kid would to a parent when they were scared. "A movie? Uh... yeah. Yeah." He held his gift shop bag hand up to offer a little shade on his face and looked over to Amber, whose ears looked like they could be sunburned, too. "Can we move to the parking garage? My car is parked there and I didn't put on sunscreen today, thinking I wouldn't be outside much."

Reuben's long, even strides were a little bit faster than a person desperately trying to leave a Walmart. Once they reached the shade, he let out a grateful breath. He let his hand fall away from Amber's and reached for his keys.

"Weird fact to know about vampires, which you might have noticed." Reuben said the 'v' word softer than the rest, as if afraid who could be listening. "We will not burst into flames like a few overexaggerated movies. We will, however, burn easily. There's a kind of sunscreen that helps us walk during the day."

Amber nodded, "I see, I see! That certainly makes a lot more sense than Hollywood. Though that's not hard...Hollywood is not known for their attention to fact." She patted Reuben's hand. "I guess I'll have to purchase a bottle of this sunscreen so I can make sure my boyfriend doesn't turn into a tomato next time."

"Please don't worry about me," Reuben insisted stubbornly. "I can handle that on my own. I was a little nervous about our first date, is all." He placed his fingers on his cheeks, his fingertips acting like little ice packs to his rosy skin. "I'm sorry. I should have taken more precautions. But the movie: I could go for whatever. Scary, comedy, romance... Whatever it is, I don't mind. I enjoy spending time with you."

Reuben made sure to dig into his pocket and at least have the door unlocked when Amber reached it. He then jogged to the other side of the car, hopping in while scanning the lot.

Amber climbed into the now-familiar black car and buckled the seat belt, feeling far more comfortable than she had the last time she was inside. As such, she took a little more time to examine the spotless interior. Was Reuben's entire life this meticulous with attention to detail?

If so, Amber made a pact to never allow Reuben to take a single step into her apartment. It was far from meticulously clean...okay, it was a disaster area. She couldn't remember the last time anyone other than Jade had been over, so there was a thick layer of 'nobody is going to see it anyway' lingering on every surface.

She found herself growing uncomfortable with the thought and cleared her throat, looking to Reuben for a change of thought trains. "I enjoy spending time with you, too. I'm glad that if I have to get out of my shell, it's with you." A genuine smile graced Amber's face as the car engine roared to life. "I'm going to pull out my phone to see what is playing, I hope you don't mind."

"Please do. I don't stay up to date with current theater movies." Reuben waited patiently while Amber searched for their options, fidgeting with the keys in his hand while trying his best not to stare.

"It looks like there are a couple of comedies, a slasher film, yet another Fast and Furious sequel, and a romance called *One Evening in Prague*." Amber's finger appeared to move on its own accord as it tapped the romance to pull up the description. It sounded like something the author would enjoy, though she eyed Reuben from the corner of her eye and cleared her throat to force her voice to function. "Would you mind watching the romance with me? For research purposes, obviously."

"One Evening in Prague, huh?" Reuben's voice was unconvinced, but he nodded in response. "I would love to. And not just for research. Romance is one of my favorite genres. I hope it's not the stereotypical, cookie cutter romance that lazy producers churn out like butter."

Amber put the phone back in her pocket and settled back into the seat. She was simply pleased to still be in the company of the handsome political figure, no matter what they decided to watch. The more time they spent together, the more she found herself attracted to Reuben.

With another side glance, she reached out and rested her hand on top of Reuben's, enjoying the sensation of the vampire's marble skin under her fingers. Her toes curled up in her shoes from happiness and she felt the muscles near her ears tighten. "It's nice to play hooky with you for a while, you know. There's something fun about knowing I'm keeping such an important man all to myself. Makes me feel like maybe I *am* more than a shut-in author with no friends pretending to date a politician."

She ran her thumb up and down Reuben's knuckles, imagining how much better this would feel if Reuben had feelings for her, too. An impossible scenario, she knew, but such was life. In the end, this whole setup would at least result in a unique and hopefully best-selling new novel. Perhaps a 'relationship of convenience to reality' trope?

Reuben's eyes shifted to their hands touching. His hand rolled over to caress Amber's warm fingers as his eyes shifted up to his date's.

"You have at least one friend, Amber: me." With a huge smile, Reuben turned his attention back to the parking garage, turned his hand back over, and put the car into drive.

Amber pulled out her notebook with her free hand and allowed it to fall open on her lap, her cheeks a lovely shade of cherry blossom. She withdrew her left hand long enough to scribble a note before returning it to its place in Reuben's.

Rather than fidgeting around to shove the notebook back in her pocket, she allowed it to remain open so she could glance through her notes. They were scattered, nonsensical, and fairly illegible to anyone else, but somehow, between the brown leather covers rested a new novel.

They pulled into a parking spot near the movie theater door. A few scattered cars spotted the parking lot, while only a handful of workers could be seen through the windows. Reuben unbuckled his seat belt after the car turned quiet. "You pay for the tickets? I pay for the snacks? I'm thinking a cherry Icee."

Amber nodded and didn't hesitate to take Reuben's hand for their short walk. She was proud to have such a kind, good-looking man by her side, even if it was tainted by their arrangement.

Before entering, Reuben placed his hand on his date's lower back, ushering her into the building as he followed close behind. The rush of cool air from the air conditioning hit his face and the muscles in his shoulders relaxed. He let out a sigh and began looking around for the ticket desk.

Amber blushed deeply as the vampire's gentle hand rested in the curve of her spine. She was surprised how natural and pleasant it felt. She, too, took a look around, though mostly to locate the snacks.

The lobby was quite empty and the marquee flashed that the romance film would begin in fifteen minutes. It almost appeared that the fates were lining things up for the faux couple. Perfect first date almost achieved!

They walked up to the ticket desk where Amber purchased two tickets to *One Evening in Prague*. The woman behind the desk looked at the pair of them strangely, but didn't say anything as she handed over the tickets and Amber's card.

Amber smiled to the ticket lady's face, but as soon as she turned around, it fell from her lips. A gross feeling swirled in her stomach as her brain recycled the image of the ticket lady's judgy expression. What was her problem? Did she notice Reuben's vampirism? Was she judging Amber's fashion sense? She grew a little anxious about who else might be judging the couple, but Reuben's calm presence helped ground her flightiness.

With tickets in hand, it was time to peruse the overpriced snacks. Faced with the entirety of the theater snack section, Amber carefully scanned the list as if she were making the most important decision of her life. "Medium popcorn and soda deal, root beer," she said, nodding contentedly.

"And a large cherry Icee for me," Reuben finished.

"Anything else?" asked the attendant.

Not seeing any lollipops or hard candies, Reuben shook his head and handed over his card. The bored teenager at the counter soon returned the card and handed over the snacks.

With the popcorn tucked in her elbow and her soda in one hand, Amber offered an empty hand to fill it...with Reuben's.

Theater Four was their destination, and after pausing for a moment at the podium to have their tickets checked, the pair made a bee-line for the proper doors. They swung open and Reuben held them open for Amber, the manners that HOME had drilled into him coming out in full force.

Not a single seat had yet been filled. "Do you think anyone else is going to be at such an early showing?" Amber asked, grabbing a bit of popcorn with her lips from the top of the container. "This has been out for a while, so I guess it would be possible for us to have the entire theater to ourselves."

"I wouldn't complain about a private showing," Reuben laughed, his eyes lighting up as he saw this theater had been equipped with comfortable recliner seats. "Sweet, I love these seats! After you, *my dear.*" Reuben followed Amber up the stairs and the couple settled in. The middle armrest could be lifted out of the way, which was an added bonus.

Reuben set his drink in the outside cupholder, in case he felt like practicing his moves later. He could be far more subtle without having to relocate the Icee first. "I think we have perfect timing. Must be fate." He relaxed back into his recliner and allowed the leg rest to go up before taking a satisfying sip of his cherry drink.

The blush returned at the pet name, but Amber grinned and settled herself into the comfortable recliner seat. She, too, placed her drink in the outside cup holder and gently put the bucket of popcorn in the seat next to her. "Fate indeed," she replied, leaning toward Reuben as the lights dimmed and the previews began to play.

Amber's hand started on the arm rest, but inched toward Reuben of its own accord. Soon they were again holding hands as comfortably as if they'd been dating for a lifetime. She couldn't help glancing to the side as the previews played, finding her stomach full of butterflies again. No, she wasn't allowed to feel like this! It was all a front, after all. No more real than the stories she wrote.

CHAPTER 14

><><>**Amber**<><><

*a*s soon as the actual film began, Amber was sucked into the cheesy, stereotypical plot and generic characters. There was something comforting and welcoming in the familiar structure, as overdone as it may appear to some people.

And she kept glancing at her date. Reuben's profile in the dim glow of the theater felt somehow softer than it did in full sun. He was... Well, gorgeous, if Amber was being honest with herself. *How could I be so lucky to have someone like Reuben at my side, even if it's only pretend? There was an entire room of eligible partners, and he chose **me***.

A soft and contented smile graced Amber's lips. She allowed her head to rest on Reuben's shoulder. She could get used to this...And Reuben didn't flinch or move away in the slightest. Instead he leaned into Amber's weight, allowing himself to relax against her warmth.

But Amber couldn't help repeating the question ad nauseam: was Reuben feeling the way she was, or was he letting the author gather data in her own way? He *seemed* to be enjoying their time together and playing the part of a perfect boyfriend flawlessly.

But did he get butterflies too? Did he get a shiver down his spine when they held hands? Amber chuckled to herself at these intrusive thoughts. This was real life, not a romance novel. This was business, not pleasure. She was being absurd.

That didn't mean she couldn't enjoy it while it lasted, though. With a cheeky grin, Amber pulled Reuben's hand over to her lap where she began massaging the cold fingers and palm. She ran her finger along the lines, traced the ridges of his knuckles, massaged the finger pads with her thumb, and generally acquainted herself with every curve and ridge. It was relaxing and soothed her need to fidget.

Reuben's eyes snapped to Amber's hands. Not bothering to be subtle, he lifted his hand until both of their arms were in the air. With his free left hand, he flipped back the arm rest that separated the two by a few inches. He then dropped Amber's hand and swung his arm over her shoulder. His porcelain fingers grazed her hair as he scooted over until their legs touched and his arm rested softly on her shoulders.

There was no resistance to his moves. Amber allowed herself to be tucked against Reuben's side with hands entwined, her eyes closed and her heart pounding in his ears. She found his slender yet firm, cool fingers wrapped around hers comforting.

Their hands rested in Amber's lap for a few minutes before an intrusive thought popped into her mind. The movement was slow and her eyes were glued to Reuben as she inched their hands closer to her face, searching for any sign of consent. When he turned and smiled, Amber's smooth lips gingerly placed a soft kiss on the back of his hand.

She then nuzzled in and rested her cheek on Reuben's chest, somehow surprised at the lack of heartbeat. *You idiot, he's a vampire. He doesn't need blood pumped through his body.* In this world of fantasy mixed with reality...she'd forgotten that Reuben was supposed to be a threat. She breathed in his vanilla-scented cologne and sighed with pleasure.

><><>Reuben<><><

*B*ut Reuben hadn't forgotten. It took everything in him to stay calm with Amber so close. Not because he was tempted to bite her; in fact, that was nowhere in the violent storm of thoughts which tore through his brain. He really only needed a few ounces of blood twice a day to keep his thirst under control, and he'd downed an extra large bag this morning just in case. Instead, a slurry of guilt, repressed memories, and confusion made everything opaque.

And on top of everything was what he could only describe as a budding forbidden crush. Amber was stuck in an awkward position of being halfway between a coworker and a girlfriend. It was especially awkward when Amber did cute things...Reuben found himself more closely examining the way his date's hair curled so gently around her ears and how her eyes sparkled when she was excited. They made his chest muscles tighten and the back of his scalp tingle pleasantly.

No, no. None of that. Relationships were nothing but pain, and this was only business. Neither of them could stab each other in the back (literally or figuratively) if Reuben never allowed himself to actually get close to her. His eyes drifted closed as a soft breath escaped his lips. *But it feels so good being close to this human...or is it being treated like one that makes me feel this way?*

The movie had hit the bottom of Reuben's priority list. There was a personalized love story happening right in front of his eyes and he struggled to see where he fit into it. Amber was going to use their experiences in her new novel, so her part was easy. The more realistic the experiences, the easier her job became.

But the more realistic it became, the more complicated Reuben's job was. On one hand, he had to ask: Did this look like an actual relationship to other people? Would this be believable if he stood in front of a jury of paparazzi? On the other...the more 'real' it was, the more likely it would be for this little crush to grow into something more.

Reuben's eyes flickered back toward the movie, not wanting to seem like a creep for staring at their conjoined hands. But it had been years since he experienced intimacy like this. Even the simplest touches woke up locked away sensations that he had been denying himself for so many years. Reuben began to wonder if dating, dating a human no less, might not be so bad. Maybe he *could* enjoy a normal life, despite his incurable condition.

One step at a time. This is the first date. Or was it the second? Third? Did either of the cafe visits count? He started to feel awful, knowing this wouldn't last no matter what date number this was. That Amber would leave once she got enough information for her new novel, and when Reuben passed for being a 'normal' person by public standards. He gave a soft squeeze to Amber's shoulders, a small side hug, enjoying the closeness while it lasted.

Unfortunately, whatever mood they'd created was ruined when Reuben's phone started to vibrate near the end of the movie. It was a simple, short vibrate, indicating he was receiving text messages. At first, it was just one. Then another one a few minutes later. And then another, and another. Their frequency started to pick up after Reuben hadn't opened any, let alone responded to them. No doubt it was his work attempting to contact him for some silly reason.

The end credits started to roll and soon the lights rose. Reuben lifted his arm up off Amber and returned his chair to an upright position. He already couldn't remember a single detail about the movie...

"Well, I enjoyed that a lot," he said. Which wasn't a lie. He enjoyed cuddling with Amber on the recliners very much. "What did you think of it?"

His mind drifted along that thought line and he could only imagine what a movie night at his home could be like. A soft blanket, a long couch where they could lay down...heck, he might pass out with his own personal Amber-shaped heated blanket pressed close to his body. He quickly shook the thought out of his head and ran his fingers over his hair, checking if it was still in place.

"I enjoyed it a lot, too," Amber replied, covertly rubbing her face while nodding and wiping her damp fingers on her pants. "It was a pretty predictable storyline, but I kind of like the knowledge that the ending is going to be happy. It's much less stressful than real life, you know? Real life is so much more complicated than that."

"If real life was as easy and adventure-filled as movies, it might be a little boring." Reuben reached out and tucked a lock of Amber's unruly hair behind her ear with a smile. After patting his pockets to check for keys, wallet and sunglasses, Reuben picked up his melted drink to throw it away, then reached into his pocket and pulled out his phone. The screen lit up to reveal 17 new text messages. He sighed. "Well, it was fun while it lasted. I'd like to do this again. Soon. Once I figure out my ever-changing work schedule, that is."

"Your schedule can screw itself," Amber grumbled as she allowed Reuben to lead her back out into the parking lot where they stood in the shade of a tree. The vampire's expression when he glanced at his phone told Amber they'd probably already pushed their luck on time (plus they were still in the sun), but that didn't stop her from raising Reuben's hand to her lips and brushing her own warm ones against the cold flesh again.

As their hands lowered, Amber sighed. "Well, I best be letting you get back to work. Call me any time, eh? You know where I am. Sort of. See you soon?" Her usual flush colored her ears as Amber turned toward the nearby bus stop which would take her home.

"Soon," Reuben chuckled. He followed Amber to the bus stop, unwilling to part just yet. Yes, his schedule was extremely demanding at times, but his empty life had been perfect for it. If Reuben was always busy, then he never needed to think about how alone he was. Now? He might have to rethink things.

They stood quietly next to each other under a tree until Amber was inside the bus, then Reuben waved his new friend goodbye. "I'll see to it that your phone number is put to good use. See you soon."

He then walked in the opposite direction toward his parked car. He was still perturbed that he couldn't drive his date home, but he understood. Amber didn't want the starving paparazzi hanging around her windows...it was only polite to respect her wishes. *And* if he didn't know where she lived, he also couldn't inadvertently lead any angry mobs to her. He hopped into his car and checked his phone.

STELLA

No one has seen you in the office today. We have a meeting later.

There's no way you're still at the aquarium.

Meeting at 3 pm in conference room 1.

Don't be late.

Did you see the text about the meeting?

MEETING AT 3PM SHARP.

Reuben DEVITO.

You better be dead, not answering your phone.

Ha, didn't mean that. But you will never see the end of Mount Paperwork if you aren't here at 3.

Seriously?

Answer your phone!

Reuben! You need to be here!

He flicked through the rest of the text messages, finding more of the same with the addition of more and more curse words as he scrolled. After a quick message to tell them he would be there, Reuben put the car in reverse and pulled out of his parking place. He had twenty minutes to get to the office, which wouldn't have been a big deal if he'd been in work attire. The tangerine shirt and jeans would make him feel almost naked in the office.

Thankfully he did have an extra button-down shirt and tie in the back, which would get him through. He caught sight of himself in the mirror and scowled. His hair was anything but perfect and his face was a mess of sunburn...that was another issue, but one he had no real solution to right now. "Everyone is going to look at me like I've grown a second head," he grumbled, checking his mirrors before pulling out onto the main road.

><><>Mr. DeVito<><><

$\mathcal{M}$r. DeVito arrived with moments to spare, netting him a few extra glances from his coworkers. He could tell they were dying to know why the immaculate vampire rep arrived looking like he'd spent the day at the beach, but no one had time to interrogate him before they began.

The meeting was long and boring like every other meeting. Mr. DeVito contributed when needed, but he believed all of the information could be conveyed with a nicely written email and saved everyone the trouble. All he could think about was his morning date and how easily Amber seemed to settle into the position of girlfriend. Had she never experienced heartbreak, or was the woman that self-assured? She blushed a lot, but when it came to actions, Amber was the braver of the two.

The Vice President of HOME finally tapped his folder on the table and walked out after all the questions were asked. The rest cleared out shortly after a stretch or gathering their things.

Mr. DeVito saw his manager approaching like a bull from the corner of his eye and headed her off at the pass. "Stella...you *know* I was working on the task I was given."

He smoothed out his collar to stall as his brain pieced today's most recent events into something sensible. But also to wait until prying ears left the room. Most of his coworkers feared Stella more than they wished to sate their curiosity about Mr. DeVito's busy morning. They cleared out faster than kids on the last day of school.

Mr. DeVito continued speaking as the door clicked closed and only the two of them remained. "I'm caught up with my work. I read the scripts for the next few press interviews, gave my notes, and returned them for revisions. I signed and initialed every paper given to me. Read every email." He fiddled with his notebook and pen as he stood in her line of fire.

"This morning, I asked the woman I met at the singles event for an official first date, like I told you I was going to. We hit it off and I believe she will be a perfect partner." He felt ashamed about the way he was talking about Amber. He wasn't saying anything bad, really, but he wasn't used to talking so candidly about someone he might like. The situation was supposed to be treated like a business transaction and he knew it, but Amber was growing on him with each minute they spent together.

Stella's lips pursed, clear as day that she was debating punishment or not. She walked past the vampire, tapping his shoulder and deciding on mercy. "Job well done, but you better not let this affect your office hours. I expect you to be on time like everyone else. Nevertheless, I hope you enjoy your time with your new girlfriend. And that you keep her safe." With that, Stella disappeared.

Mr. DeVito sat at his desk the rest of the day with his tail tucked between his legs and head hung low. He tried desperately to get through the day free of questions. Despite his coworker's curious stares as they walked by, he did seem to be safe from further interrogations. He kept his head buried in work until the last person left the office. Only then did he leave, not wanting to be accused of not pulling his weight. After all the exhaustion, he passed out the second his head hit the pillow that night.

CHAPTER 15

><><>**Amber**<><><

The ride home was quiet and uneventful...and lonely. Which was an emotion Amber had felt before, but it was different now. In the past, she'd embraced the loneliness as an old friend which came with the territory of her solitary lifestyle. But now? It didn't feel quite so comfortable.

Could it be that her perfect life *was* missing something?

Scenes of their picture-perfect date danced around in her mind to a slow waltz and her inspiration ran the strongest it had ever been. Was it possible that she could have experienced this high earlier? What had she passed on by pushing everyone away for so long?

Well, that was the past and nothing could be done about it. Her time would be better spent imagining all the cute things she could do with Reuben on their next date. And the next. And the next. Her heart jumped for joy in her chest and her fingers itched for the keyboard.

The rest of the afternoon and evening were quiet. Amber made herself a cup of tea and munched on popcorn as she sat at the computer and began working again on her novel. A million thoughts swirled in her head, though few made it onto the page before night fell and she decided to go to bed. Her dreams were a jumble of nonsensical scenes with an overarching feeling of excitement that she couldn't quite place.

As usual, morning had dawned long before Amber's eyes creaked open. She stumbled out of bed into the kitchen in her bathrobe with bedhead and squinty eyes. Out of pure muscle memory she put the kettle on for her morning cocoa, opened her laptop, made a piece of toast, and sat down for her routine breakfast.

Her brain wasn't quite as awake as her body, because when she opened her internet browser and the trending articles popped up, she had to read the headlines and stare at the photo for a long time before it registered what she was seeing. *"Vito Vying for Human Vote?"* the headline read in bold, black letters. Beneath it was a photograph of herself with her lips pressed to Reuben's hand in the parking lot of the movie theater.

Her immediate reaction was an icy cold bucket of anxiety dumped on her head, which soaked into her spine and stomach. How? How had the media gotten this photograph?! Had they been followed? If so, for how long? She forced herself to calm down and read the rest of the article.

Reuben DeVito, the public face of HOME, was spotted yesterday afternoon attending a movie with a yet-unknown woman. Our journalists were able to capture this photograph thanks to a tip received from an anonymous source at the theater who spotted the two entering the building together, holding hands.

We were able to get an exclusive interview on the subject with Alexander Hawthorne, DeVito's election opponent. "It's obvious he's trying to win the human vote," Hawthorne told our reporter. "There's no way someone like DeVito would date a human. This whole thing has to be staged. Vampire Vito has never shown any romantic interest in his entire career, so why start now when the election is projected to be so close? The timing and setup is much too convenient."

The identity of the woman is yet to be discovered, but it is expected that DeVito won't keep the secret for long. Sources in-the-know suspect that he will be bringing his new partner to HOME's yearly alliance gala in June. We

Amber slammed the laptop shut and angrily sipped at her drink. Slander!! How many people would read and believe this garbage?! Well...Hawthorne wasn't wrong. Reuben really *was* pretending to date Amber to better his ratings in the polls, and had been quite frank and open about it.

So why did it make Amber feel so utterly furious seeing it in black and white? And who had called the paparazzi on them? She thought back on the few people they'd seen at the theater, mentally crossing them off until she remembered the look the ticket lady had given them. Could it be she wasn't judging them as a couple, but had recognized Reuben instead? That bitch!!

She pulled out her phone with half a mind to call Reuben, but paused. Who was she mad at, anyway? It wasn't like Reuben set them up. His phone had been in his pocket the entire time, the movie hadn't been planned...there was no way he could have been behind the spotting. Was it instead that she was upset, and her instinct was to call her boyfriend? Well, that was new.

This was a crossroads. No amount of warning could have prepared the squirrely author to see her picture in the news. Everything in her logical brain screamed that it was time to abandon ship before someone linked her with her pen name (as if literally anything about her face or name would do so.)

And a week ago, it wouldn't have been a question. She would have been out faster than popcorn on the stove without a lid. But her more primal emotions soothed the fear like a mother's touch, slowing her racing heart as she remembered how she felt when their hands intertwined. Whichever way she chose, there was no turning back.

With her head still spinning, Amber did her best to bury herself in writing as a distraction. "You're such an idiot," she muttered as her middle finger again slammed the backspace button. "Just call him! Or at least text him. Quit being such a baby! Useless, pathetic, anxiety-ridden-"

Then Amber's ranting was interrupted by the sound of "Vampires Will Never Hurt You" playing from her phone.

><><>Reuben<><><

*T*hat morning, Reuben woke to his phone vibrating itself around the nightstand. At first he thought it was his alarm, but the sounds were too constant. He rolled over, ripped his phone off the nightstand, and peeked at the blinding screen with one eye open.

A groan escaped his lips at seeing dozens of different notifications. Phone calls, text messages, news headlines...they weren't making sense to his fuzzy brain, but all told the same story.

Reuben and Amber had been caught.

He shot out of bed like he had been hit by lightning, his eyes scanning over every word of every notification.

> ERIN
>
> Are the headlines true?
>
> LUNA
>
> Wow Reuben! She's so cute!
>
> You have to let me meet her!
>
> ERIN
>
> You aren't feeding off her, are you?

And the most important one from Stella.

> STELLA
>
> So you weren't lying, Reuben. Good work.
> She's very cute.

His eyes froze on the picture that had been snapped of the two of them under the theater's tree. It was lovely in the moment. Reuben had believed the two of them were in their own little world, but reality came back to bite him in the butt.

Once Reuben reached the end of the notifications, he realized that

Amber hadn't messaged him. His night owl writer wasn't a morning person, which meant she might not have been awake yet. She might not have seen the news.

Hopefully she just hadn't seen?

><><>Mr. DeVito<><><

*M*r. DeVito was treated like he had already won the election as he walked into the office. The gossip ranged from quiet whispers behind his back to shameless questions. The goal had been publicity, and boy was he getting it!

But he could only think about the lack of response from Amber.

The other down side was that PR pulled him into meetings for most of the morning. Discussions ranged from how the news story was both the best and the worst thing that had ever happened, to whether the stunt should be repeated. They would have to schedule a meeting with the press to get in front of the situation either way. Mr. DeVito would address issues or concerns with the people, while keeping the true arrangement a secret.

After intense rounds of 'how do we spin this,' PR decided on rolling with the relationship being fresh and that the annual supernatural/human singles event was a huge success this year, bringing species closer together. Mr. DeVito went to support the cause and fell for someone. It wasn't that far from the truth and might bring greater publicity for future events.

It was noon before Reuben got a free minute. He hadn't had a second to send a text asking how Amber was taking the lack of privacy. Fortunately, cameras weren't allowed inside of a movie theater or they might have gotten a deeper look into their budding partnership. The media would also use any sort of misinformation if it made them a dollar.

Reuben had been hoping he could introduce Amber to the world of paparazzi in a more controlled setting; but to be fair, it could have gone much worse. The paparazzi could've run up to them with hundreds of deeply personal questions without shame. Or the title could have been *"Vampire Vito Enslaves New Blood Bag."* And there weren't even any angry mobs throwing rocks at his office window.

He used his lunch to hide himself in his empty office, blinds drawn shut and the door closed. Not a single soul would bother him on his break; he would make sure of it. He picked up his phone again, a frown forming on his face when he still didn't see a single message from Amber.

His entire day had been spent thinking about the woman and how to make it up to her, yet Amber hadn't said a thing? The vampire's finger hovered over the call button, fearing that she would cut all ties after the news article. It took a while, but Reuben bit the bullet and pressed the call button.

"Hey sweetheart," Amber answered.

"Hey- uh. I... did you... have you seen the news yet?" Reuben rubbed his forehead roughly, cursing himself for not coming up with words before calling. An audible sigh escaped his stressed lips.

"Oh, yeah. I did see that."

"I'm so sorry. I didn't mean for that to happen. I, well. I'm sorry." Reuben couldn't think of anything else to say. No amount of explaining the situation would get him out of this mess. He already felt like he had failed his girlfriend even though he made it clear that paparazzi would be involved. Was it too soon, though? Yesterday was their first time in public and it had already proven that cameras followed Reuben no matter where he went.

But now that the news was out, people would be looking at him and the unknown girlfriend's relationship under a microscope. Reuben waited not-so-patiently for Amber's response as his foot tapped wildly against the floor. "Maybe I should've worn a fake mustache."

He laughed as the mental stress cracked his armor. It wasn't funny. Okay, Reuben in a terrible fake mustache would have been funny, but this wasn't the time to make jokes. As his awkward laughter died down, his tone turned to a more solemn, gentle one. "Are you okay? Can I do anything to make it up to you?"

"Hey, hey. It's alright, honey. It's not like you set it up or anything!

And I think you'd need more than a fake mustache to throw off the media. I'll be fine, I swear. As far as I know, the drama-sucking, buzzing pests didn't follow me home, so you've kept up your end of the bargain already.

"You know, it's probably a good thing they caught me kissing your hand, or imagine the comments the article would be getting! There would probably have been a much higher percentage throwing a fit about 'taking advantage of humans' if the roles had been swapped."

The thought felt like a mouthful of mud being shoved down Reuben's throat. He had to admit that Amber was right. If the media had snapped a photo with the vampire's mouth too close to any human body part, they may start to get other ideas. The headline could also have been infinitely nastier for Reuben's career if one of the more extreme political papers had been called. Their little local paper was fairly center of the spectrum, so they'd lucked out this time.

However, he knew that now that the word was out, they'd have to prepare for far more slanderous pieces to crop up. Reuben already feared the media would see his new friend as a victim, which was one reason he was so careful about consent. Or what if they didn't see her as a victim, but a traitor? "Don't worry too much about the reaction of the public. That's my problem, not yours. And stay out of the comment sections, okay?"

"I totally haven't been stalking the comments on the online version of the article...at all. Not a little bit. But if I had been reading them, I'm sure I would have also seen them going on and on about how lucky you are to have such a cute girlfriend. Along with the wave who agree with the title, but I suppose that means that our plan is working. We'll ignore the ones insisting that you must have hypnotized me or something."

Reuben raised an eyebrow, curious as to why Amber would be subjecting herself to the comments section at all. He knew reading all the faceless remarks was absolutely aggravating. So many people proudly spewed hate when they were safe behind a screen. It was quite surprising that Amber could come out of that flood with a smile on her face.

Rather than worry about it, Reuben teased, "They did get one thing right. The girl in the photo with me was pretty cute. I wish I had a better picture than one taken in secret." A soft chuckle accompanied the shameless compliment, but soon faded away. "Just…read those comments with a grain of salt. Don't let their rude comments get to you."

"We'll have to take a picture on our next date! But don't worry. I'm used to comment sections. I'm a romance author, after all! Let me tell you, those reviews are all over the freaking place. Unhinged soccer moms with unhappy marriages are the worst. Actually, no. My agent Gabriella is the worst."

Reuben leaned against the wall and closed his eyes as Amber spoke. "I can't believe how calm you are with all of this. I expected you would be having a meltdown. I'm impressed."

"I had my meltdown already. You missed it! But I guess nothing bad has happened yet, and freaking out would only make me miserable. So I'm doing my best to remain as cool as I ever get."

"I suppose that's true, and I appreciate it," Reuben replied. "Though you said the words 'our next date.' I would love that. What were you thinking? Maybe a picnic hike? Painting mugs? Sunset beach campfire? A trip to the zoo? Cozy movie night at my house?"

He could have gone on and on about all the things he would like to do with Amber; even though their relationship was pretend, he finally had someone to accompany him to all the silly places he wanted to go.

"I would love every single one of those ideas. Though it might be a little early to…"

She trailed off and Reuben found the silence a bit nerve wracking, until she began again. "Nah, not too early. I think all of those ideas would be perfect."

Reuben was pleased by the answer, but knew they hadn't gotten through all the hard bits yet. "I promise to be a gentleman, no matter our next move." He didn't know which idea Amber had second thoughts about, but he assumed it was one that left them alone together. Though Amber seemed to have no problems with Reuben being a vampire, there were still the countless stories, movies and preconceived notions that the public had towards them.

"We do have to be extra careful now…I don't want the vultures chasing you home and ambushing you outside your front door. I'd feel terrible if I left you to deal with that by yourself. At least if I was there, I'd be able to fight them off for you."

"I appreciate that. I've managed to avoid having to learn how to deal with them thus far. But perhaps I'll have to take some lessons, because I'm sure they'll find me alone at some point. So...what happens from here, though? I have no doubt that the media is going to get their answers whether we give them or whether they have to dig them up. But I don't know how to deal with fame other than hiding in my house. Hence the pen name…

"But I also should ask, are you okay? You're the one who has more to lose in this situation. I'm a nobody. Do you think we were convincing enough? I guess it was a good thing we've been 'practicing' when we thought nobody was looking. Or maybe that got us into trouble. Would there have been so much of a scandal if we'd looked like casual friends going to a film? Does this qualify as a scandal?"

What *did* happen from here? Reuben chuckled at yet another round of Amber's rambling, but quickly frowned and leaned forward in his chair. Would it be awkward to ask for a text message when Amber arrived home? Was it too early to ask her to spend the night on late dates so she could leave during the daylight hours, lessening her chance of being caught off guard?

"I'm a little stressed, but I'll be okay." He bit his bottom lip, considering if they *had* been convincing enough. It bothered him that he really didn't know. The man who could come up with an answer to everything had been stumped twice in one conversation. Yes, he loved romance novels, but this was real life. What were the expectations of a new couple?

"You play the part well, Amber," Reuben assured, figuring he could say at least that much. "The only scandal committed is showing the public that I could ever find love in the condition that I am. About the media, though...I have been scheduled to address the press in an hour. I've been instructed to keep it short, sweet, and to not answer questions afterwards."

"Perhaps I should have been an actor instead of an author! And if that's a scandal, then the definition needs to be changed. Because not being allowed to find love based on any trait is unacceptable. Everyone deserves to find love if that's what they want. People are so ridiculous."

"I agree. And like you said, they will find information about us, but I am not going to use your name or anything personal. The short sweet version? I went to support an interspecies singles night, found someone and went on a couple of dates afterwards."

Reuben hated how cold it sounded. He could have melted hearts with the cootie-filled details, but even if Stella hadn't given specific instructions, Reuben wanted their shared moments to be the two of them. Amber was there to act like his girlfriend to the public, yes, but he didn't want to wave her around. He didn't enjoy feeling like a zoo animal being watched from a camera lens and doubted that Amber did, either.

"I suppose there's no way around it. Maybe slip in a comment about her wanting to maintain her peaceful private life? I doubt it'll deter the slathering mongrels, but it would make me feel a little better."

Reuben assured her, "I will make sure to ask for privacy in the nicest way possible. I'm doubtful that they will listen, though." He rubbed his chin, knowing asking the wrong way could be problematic. The public might think he was trying to hide an ever darker secret behind their relationship.

"You mind if I use that, though? Everyone deserves to find love? You kind of summarized it perfectly and I think the media will love it." The vampire's thoughts got tugged back into thinking about work and the looming press conference. A soft sigh escaped his lips as he thought about the camera sharks once more.

"I'm down for more practice," Amber admitted. "I...I want to spend more time with you. Which is something I'm completely baffled about, because I've never wanted to spend time with anyone before."

A feeling of heat began spreading through Reuben's veins and a smile spread across his marble cheeks. "That's great! We'll plan something for the next time I can manage to get away. I also need to talk to you about one more thing: the gala. I had intended to talk to you about it later, but the idiot press stole my thunder."

Reuben growled a little, but knew there was nothing to be done about it now. "It'll be a black tie event and I thought…maybe we could go together, and perhaps we should have matching outfits. Not that you weren't absolutely *ravishing* at the singles event, but I want to make sure that my woman turns heads. Those reporters calling you a nobody need to be put in their place." The thought of formalwear shopping was to die for if it was with Amber, even if he had to explain the expense to Stella.

There was a long pause, and Reuben began to worry he was going to be hung up on. But thankfully, he eventually heard Amber's voice rather than a dial tone.

"Yes, I would like to go with you. Would you mind if I get a suit, too? Dresses aren't exactly my thing. And ten-year-old brown tweed doesn't exactly scream 'black tie,' if you know what I mean. At this point, the only heads turning would be turning to wonder who let this underdressed idiot through the door."

"Oh hush. They already think you're gorgeous, and that was in a parking lot with casual clothing. They haven't seen you all dressed up yet. And hey, the tweed wasn't bad. I thought you looked lovely." Reuben knew it wouldn't pass black tie standards, but he couldn't help slipping in compliments whenever he could. "Are you sure you want a suit, though? There are options between a dress and a suit these days."

Amber wrinkled her nose. "If you're worried that I'll be bothered by what people at the gala will say about me showing up in a suit, don't. I've heard it all. But just because I haven't transitioned doesn't mean I don't want to feel handsome sometimes."

Reuben was momentarily taken aback as he processed what Amber was really telling him. "Oh! I see. Thank you for trusting me with that. If you want a suit, you can have a suit! I have a shop I always go to when I need a new one. They are super nice and their work is top notch. And Bryce won't even bat an eye, I know it. Why don't we set up a fitting soon? And…would you prefer I call you handsome instead of lovely?"

"At this point, I'm not overly bothered either way. I'm still figuring things out, you know? I appreciate the ask, though. And my calendar says that other than dinner with my parents on Sundays, I'm all yours whenever you want me. Er...whenever you have time."

Reuben smirked as Amber tripped over her words. 'He could have Amber whenever he wanted?' The thought of it sent shivers down his spine. How was this woman making Reuben's walls fall with such little effort? Before he could say anything else, their phone call was interrupted by a banging on his door, signaling that he'd already taken more time than he should have.

><><>**Amber**<><><

*A*mber heard the irate knocking and shouts of 'Get your butt out here before you miss the press conference, or I'll string your head up on the front desk to welcome visitors for the rest of eternity!' after which the phone went dead. She laughed, flopped back onto the couch, and couldn't help but grin from ear to ear.

A second date! Or third if coffee counted, but the more time she spent with Reuben, the more she wanted to count every minute. She knew the end of this relationship was going to be more painful the more fully she allowed herself to get attached. But that didn't stop her from realizing that she was falling, and fast.

What if...she did her best to make him fall, too?

CHAPTER 16

><><>Mr. DeVito<><><

"Hello, everyone. Thank you for coming today on such short notice." Mr. DeVito looked straight into the crowd of cameras and microphones. He held his head high with a strong set of shoulders, hair perfectly placed and back ramrod straight. If Mr. Vito was agitated, not a single person in the room knew. He looked confident, brave, and happy to be there. "I'm here to address an article that was released earlier today with a picture of me and a woman."

The crowd of reporters grew loud and the flashing of their cameras threatened to blind him, but Mr. DeVito maintained an aura of calm. "I attended a lovely HOME-sponsored singles event a couple of weeks ago to show my support for the cause. Unexpectedly, I fell for one of the other participants and have since been dating her. Yes, she is a human woman, but that doesn't lessen the feelings I have towards her. Love isn't dependent on one's physical traits and shouldn't be frowned upon because we are so different.

"As my running mate, Alexander Hawthorne, has stated, this relationship could not have come at a more unfortunate time. However, I believe we can all agree that no one ever plans on meeting their special person. I do intend to give my professional and social life equal amounts of dedication moving forward.

"I have no ill will toward Mr. Hawthorne or the reporter who released the article that I am sure most of you have seen. Many still don't understand that supernatural beings have emotions the same as any human would. The last few years, I have spent my time dedicated to bringing supernaturals and humans closer together so that we may live in harmony and benefit from each other's strengths. This new partnership is a fruit of HOME's labor and shows the reality of their main goal: *cohabitating peacefully together.*

"I hope everyone will see how happy we make each other, but I do ask that we receive some privacy as we navigate our budding relationship. I will not be answering any questions today, but I will not keep the media in the dark. I appreciate everyone coming. Thank you."

Mr. DeVito gave a big smile as the cameras continued furiously snapping. The crowd's volume rose exponentially as he stepped away from the podium, sticking to his word that he would not answer any questions. Many called his name or yelled questions anyway, hoping to squeeze any information they could from him.

He was guided out of the room by security and taken back to his office as the media cleared out of the press room. But Mr. DeVito had no time to breathe before the PR team dragged him back into another long meeting to go over the release.

><><>Amber<><><

*A*s much as she despised the news, Amber's heart pounded as the face of her boyfriend appeared on the screen. The hoard of reporters could be seen crowding the platform he stood on and flashes of cameras turned the scene into a technological lightning storm. However, Reuben looked calm and composed as he began to speak.

His words were sweet to Amber's ears, despite knowing they were a work of fiction. "You're totally convincing," Amber told the TV, a soft smile on her face. She couldn't pull her eyes away from that handsome, sharp face that just yesterday had been inches away from her own.

The roar of the crowd as Reuben stepped away blasted through Amber's computer speakers and she hurriedly muted it. She didn't want to click out of the tab until Reuben had disappeared from the screen and a sigh slipped through her teeth.

The news station's reporter appeared on the screen and she unmuted the speakers, curious what they'd have to say. It seemed she only caught the tail end, however. *"Whether this is truthful or a publicity stunt by HOME is yet to be seen. This is Cecilia Hope, Channel 5 News."*

All the warm fuzzies that she'd been feeling went out the window. Amber slammed the tab closed and pushed her office chair away from the desk. Publicity stunt?! Okay, well...maybe it was. But they weren't supposed to say things like that! She paced around her small apartment until the annoyance subsided, then pulled out her phone and opened Reuben's contact.

AMBER

You did really well, handsome.

She waited a long time for a reply before sighing and putting the phone away. Surely Reuben had been whisked away for a neverending cycle of meetings or something, right? Amber shook the hair from her eyes and headed to the worst possible place to waste time: social media comment sections.

While the comments on the news article had been moderately annoying, Amber had breezed through them unscathed. The press release brought out a different variety of internet troll, however. Each comment of "can anyone make out her face?", "does anyone recognize the girl?", and "I bet 4Chan already has the girl's full doxx" poured fear directly into Amber's stomach until the whites of her eyes were exposed in panic.

She scoured site after site, digging into the underbelly of the internet to ensure nobody had figured out her identity. Darkness fell over the faded yellow wallpaper and beige carpet, only being kept at bay by the flickering glow of the computer screen as it switched from page to page to page.

*I*t was well after office hours before Reuben was free to go. He hadn't had a day at work like that in a while. He usually kept his nose out of trouble, so dealing with PR scandals wasn't a common occurrence.

Of course, the HOME leadership wanted to go over what would happen in the future and when Reuben could bring Amber into the office. He did manage to get them to back off the idea, though it took all of his debate skills. It was true that nothing bad could happen behind their security, but Amber was her own person. She wasn't a prisoner.

Reuben tugged his phone out to contact Amber before he left the office.

REUBEN

Just finished work. I wanted to talk to you again. It's refreshing.

I was wondering if you wanted to stop by my house for a movie some time?

It would be private and you could spend the night if it gets too late.

Not that I would be expecting anything because it was private.

Not that I wouldn't want to…you know, with you.

I mean, not that I want to, either.

I meant private so we wouldn't feel like the fish at the aquarium.

My apologies. My brain is fried.

The more Reuben typed, the deeper the hole he dug for himself. This was the exact reason his speeches were structured and planned out. He felt like a fool for texting Amber as the sun had already dipped below the horizon. It was late, by human standards.

Reuben didn't know when Amber's official bedtime was, but he hoped he could at least talk to his girlfriend over the phone for a few minutes before they both went to sleep. Anything to take his mind off the exhausting day he had at work.

He drove to his house and stopped at the security gate that protected his neighborhood from unwanted visitors. While it was mostly an affluent human area, Reuben felt comfortable in his little slice of the world. He mentioned he might be having company over at some point and wrote Amber's name on his acceptable visitor list. The gates opened, allowing Reuben to drive through.

The second he got home, he had a small blood bag as a snack and then took one of the hottest showers in his life. The water melted away hours of stress that settled in his muscles. He then spent extra time brushing his teeth and gargling the smell of pennies away. Just because Reuben drank blood didn't mean he had to smell like it.

Realizing he hadn't bothered to check his mail for a week or so, Reuben put on a bathrobe and slippers to walk to the corner. He unlocked the door to his mailbox and found a little package inside. Curious, he pulled it out and tucked it under his arm. One more peek showed the mailbox was empty.

Once he was back inside, Reuben placed the package on the counter and went searching for a pair of scissors. "Ah, there you are!" he exclaimed to the inside of a drawer and pulled out the desired tool. He carefully cut open the top of the bubble envelope and pressed the sides so he could see the contents.

And immediately flung himself back, sending the package tumbling into his sink. Light reflected on the sharp metal needle of a syringe, half filled with a cloudy liquid. Written in sharpie on a piece of tape stuck to the syringe were three words: we found you.

><><>Amber<><><

*T*he author sat on her couch with her laptop, still feverishly scrolling through social media. Every other post was either the news article, the press release, or some sort of meme created about the situation, but her name still hadn't been posted anywhere. She wanted to discuss the problem with Reuben, but her text had still gone unanswered.

As she was considering starting a pity-party movie marathon which would inevitably have kept her up *far* too late, her phone began to vibrate. Amber pounced on it and groaned with relief when Reuben's name appeared on the screen.

She'd started to type out a reply when another text came in, then another, and another, causing Amber to begin laughing. She waited a couple of minutes after the final message to make sure there weren't any more coming before typing her own response. They were endearing; the awkward pit-digging was such a juxtaposition to the calm and collected Reuben who had stood in front of all those cameras.

AMBER

I'd be happy to come to your house sometime if you are willing to give me your address. I don't know if I'm ready to stay over yet, but I guess we'll see what happens.

But speaking of addresses, I really need to talk to you about some of the comments I saw after the press release.

I plead the fifth on wanting anything.

The little 'typing' bubbles started and stopped repeatedly at the bottom of Amber's screen, as if Reuben couldn't decide what to say. The author reclined on the sofa and watched them dance until the phone began to ring instead. "Hello?"

"Hello, my dear Gem. What did I tell you about reading the

comment sections? Nothing good comes out of those. You're better off not giving them the time of day."

Amber grew annoyed, shaking her head despite knowing Reuben couldn't see it. "It isn't the comments themselves that are the problem. The whole internet is after my doxx, Reuben. I've been searching all day for any sign that they've figured out who I am and where I live. I didn't expect that the first day they'd jump to trying to find me! And after the press release, comments started popping up about 'finding the blood bank and straightening her out.' I feel like I'm being hunted!" The more she spoke, the more frantic Amber's voice became.

"Gem. Gem! GEM! Calm down, everything will be fine. Breathe, okay? I will call HOME's PR team and get them working on a distraction, okay? I promised that your address would be safe and I meant it. Nobody is going to find you. Just turn off the social media before it makes you crazy. I know it's late, but do you want to meet me at our coffee shop as a distraction? I can get PR activated and then we can talk this out in person."

Amber felt like the room was spinning. She closed the laptop and her eyes, trying to sip from the fountain of comfort Reuben was offering to little avail. "Not tonight," she said, trying to stem her anger that he continued to focus on her reading of the comments, not her actual fears. "I don't dare leave my apartment tonight. Tomorrow?"

"Okay. I'll make tomorrow work. The earliest I can be there is five-thirty. Would that work for you?"

"Yeah. I'll see you then." Without giving Reuben a chance to say anything else, Amber hung up the phone and tossed it to the far end of the couch. "It's not his fault," she explained to the empty room. The fear slowly cooled to a glowing ember of anger which she hunkered next to, unwilling to let it go out.

CHAPTER 17

><><>**Amber**<><><

*A*mber fidgeted with the handle of her cocoa mug and glanced again at the clock on the wall. 5:35. Her lips tightened. It wasn't like Reuben to be late. Was he not coming? The author sipped the last of her cocoa and pushed away the cup, which Marissa whisked away moments later.

"Would you like anything else while you wait, pudding?" Marissa gave Amber a genuine smile and tilted her head, an auburn curl falling from her shoulder. The author shook her head and she nodded. "Alright. I'll be around if you change your mind! A little odd for that boyfriend of yours to be late, isn't it?"

Amber nodded, chewing on the inside of her cheek nervously. "Yeah. Super odd. Hopefully everything is okay."

Marissa agreed and moved along to the only other occupied table in the cafe, leaving Amber to wallow in the sea of 'what ifs' which whipped up to massive waves that stole her breath with every new crash. She scooted back on her red-upholstered chair and folded her arms on the table, then placed her chin on top while staring out the window.

The sun hadn't reached the horizon yet, but overzealous street lights were flickering to life while shift workers hurried by on their way home. Amber watched these droop-shouldered and solemn-faced men and women speed walk right past the little cafe without giving it a single glance. They were so engrossed in their own lives that more than once someone would bump into another passerby going in the other direction, jolting both away from their public solitude for a brief moment.

Were she and Reuben the same? Just two people knocked out of their isolation for only a fleeting instant?

Then the bell above the door tinkled and in walked the missing vampire. His eyes were wide and wild, though his posture and hair maintained their usual level of poise. Marissa nodded pleasantly to Reuben as he passed the counter and sat down across from Amber, a million excuses clinging to his lips.

"The usual, please," Reuben requested in the barista's direction, turning back to his date as soon as she acknowledged him. "Amber, I am so sorry! It's out of my character to be late, but with all the mess from yesterday, I didn't want to give away our secret spot. I parked my car about a mile away and misjudged how long it would take to sneak here without using my speed."

Amber glanced down at her hands, the corners of her lips twitching as if arguing whether to go up or down. Down won and when the author finally made eye contact with the vampire, dejection dampened her aura.

Reuben curled his toes and reached out to take Amber's hands, but she pulled them out of reach. "Amber, I really am sorry that I'm late. I wanted to keep the paparazzi and protestors off our trail."

A visible flinch followed the word 'paparazzi,' and Amber collapsed in on herself a little before speaking. "I'm not upset that you were late," she said, voice barely above a whisper. "I'm freaked out about the comments calling for me to be doxxed or worse, and the fact that you had to go to such lengths to ditch the press. And I'm upset that you brushed that all off so easily." She peeked up through her eyebrows with haunted eyes.

"I didn't mean to," Reuben sighed, melting into his own chair and unbuttoning his jacket. "I guess I'm so used to dodging them that it's second nature to me. But if it makes you feel better, nobody has posted your name anywhere so far. And the public has such a short attention span, I bet they'll have moved on to the next thing by Friday." Reuben again reached out to cup Amber's cheek.

This time she didn't move; she allowed the porcelain fingers to caress her face. But before Amber could formulate a reply or assess how she was feeling, her phone began ringing loudly. She kept her ringtone loud due to the small number of calls she received and smaller amount of time she spent in public, so hearing it blasting through the cafe caused her to scramble.

She nearly dropped the phone in her haste to stop the sound, but managed to catch and silence it. The screen displayed Jade's name, which did nothing to lower her anxiety. "I'm sorry, it's my sister. She rarely calls, so I better take this." Without further explanation, Amber scooted out the front door of the cafe and leaned against the wall. "Hello?"

"Hey Amby, where are you? I stopped by your apartment to drop off some stuff that mom pulled out of a closet and decided you needed, but I guess you're not home."

Relief crept in to take the place of the anxiety. "Oh, that's all? I was worried you were calling to tell me Dad is in the hospital again or something. I'm over at the coffee shop."

"The usual one?"

"Yeah, the regular one. I'll be a little while. Do you want to leave the stuff on the doorstep?"

"Do you WANT it to get stolen? I know how sketchy that apartment building of yours is. I'll use my spare key to go inside and put it on the table."

"What is it? I might not even want it. We both know how Mom is...she can't throw anything away. If it's something stupid again like my homework from first grade or a rock I picked up in middle school, put it in the dumpster." She rubbed her eyes in some attempt to relax the irritation which had settled into her bones.

A glance through the coffee shop window showed that the barista was headed toward her table with Reuben's drink and another cocoa she figured he'd ordered for her, so she groaned. "Otherwise, fine, leave it on the table. I have to go. Reuben and I need to finish our conversation."

"WHO IS REUBEN?"

Jade's voice and question were cut off abruptly as Amber realized she'd slipped. She hung up as fast as possible and jammed her phone into her pocket, ignoring the further buzzes of multiple text messages. It was only a few steps to the table where a new cup of cocoa steamed, a heavenly combination of mint and almond drifting toward her.

Amber slid back into her chair and gave Reuben an apologetic smile. "Sorry about that. I thought maybe something had gone wrong with Dad, but it was my sister telling me she was at my apartment to drop some stuff off." She picked up her cup and sniffed, eyes half closing from exhaustion.

"Oh no. Don't worry about it. Glad it wasn't anything too serious. I thought I'd buy you another cocoa, since I was late and you already finished yours." Reuben fidgeted with his spoon and said, "So about the press thing. It will be alright, I promise. This wasn't as controlled as I would have hoped, but so far everything I've seen has been positive. Even the ones who are wondering who you are. PR has been hard at work keeping things under control, too."

Amber stirred her cup moodily, eyes still dark. She felt that she had two options: spiral into a panic and never leave her apartment again, or allow herself to trust that Reuben would keep his word and keep her safe. As she stared at the handsome man across the table, the fear melted away a little and the second option felt a little more possible.

Despite the serious nature of their conversation, the buzzing of Amber's phone was incredibly distracting to both parties. "You sure that's not important? Usually just dropping something off doesn't take that many messages," Reuben murmured, pointing to Amber's pocket. "I don't mind if you need to take a call. I understand."

"Oh, everything is fine. I *was* worried about Dad for a second. He's old and sometimes ends up in the hospital for minor things, but not this time. Really don't worry about it!"

Reuben didn't look convinced, but he didn't try to fight Amber any harder on the topic. "If you're sure. We really need to talk about your comment section problem. You keep telling me that you can handle it, but all of the stress you've been feeling comes from those faceless posts. If you'd just ignore them, you would be so much happier."

The ember of anger that Amber had been cradling immediately burst back into full flame. "You and your harping on my social media usage! Who do you think you are, my father? It's really none of your business what I choose to spend my time doing! Especially when I'm just covering my back and making sure I'm not blindsided by crazy people on the internet finding my address!"

"None of my business?!" Reuben spat, his hand curling into a fist. "After I've spent the last 24 hours making sure you had nothing to worry about, you tell me it's *none of my business?* I've told you over and over that I will make sure nobody gets your information because of our arrangement, but obviously you don't trust me! Why are you so paranoid, anyway?!"

Before Amber could reply, their conversation was cut short by the sound of the front door flying open and Amber's name being screeched through the coffee shop. All four people inside swiveled their heads to stare at the short, brown-haired and brown-eyed woman who had emitted the terrible sound. She stormed over to Amber and immediately punched her in the shoulder, her face full of unbridled irritation.

"Amber Jane Marcus!!" she shrieked again, "how dare you hang up on me and then *COMPLETELY IGNORE MY TEXTS?* You can't just mention *A MAN* cryptically and not explain yourself!"

Jade took a deep breath and looked at Reuben, an entirely different voice coming from her. "Hello, I'm Jade. You must be the other half of 'our'!"

Reuben's eyes shot to the noise and followed the young lady screaming Amber's *full* name. He didn't move to protect Amber, even when she got punched. "Yes, my apologies if I am keeping her from you," he said instead, standing from his chair to bow politely.

"This is Reuben. He's helping me with my next book." Amber rubbed her sore arm and pouted at her older sister, who was sliding herself into the bench next to her. "How did you get here so fast, anyway?"

Jade rested her elbows on the table and her chin on her hands, looking Reuben up and down with bright eyes. "Luck, really. I was on the way back to your place when I called, and only two blocks away from here," she replied, not even glancing at her sister.

Don't you dare start interrogating him, you little pest, Amber thought, feeling a small amount of panic beginning to fill her gut. There was no way she would have let Jade meet Reuben this early.

Jade paid little attention to Amber's obvious discomfort. She was instead showing deep interest in Reuben. He, in turn, made sure to sit up straight and stare right back at her. "Reuben, is it? Nice to meet you. So are you secretly a romance author as well? It took a long time for me to convince Amby to publish-"

She was cut short by Amber smacking her and shaking her head with wide eyes. Jade raised one eyebrow and sighed at her sister, somehow understanding what she wasn't saying. "Ah. You haven't given your friend here your pen name, have you? Good grief, Amby. You've got to get over that at some point. Let people know how amazing you are! And stop going out in public in your pajamas, yeah? Take a leaf from your friend's book. He seems to know how to dress himself." She turned her head back to Reuben and shot him a beaming smile, which looked a whole lot like her sister's.

"Thank you for the compliment, but Amber doesn't need to dress up to look pretty," Reuben replied with a frown and Jade shrugged, the pair again locked in a staring contest as if they were each trying to read the other's mind.

Amber didn't notice. She was at war with herself. As much as she wanted to continue her fight with Reuben, she also wanted to get Jade away from her boyfriend as fast as possible. This was too much too fast, and she could feel her blood pressure rising with each passing moment.

"Well Reuben, I shouldn't keep you too much longer," Amber said, a bit too loudly. "I know you need to get home and I need to get back to writing. We are going to have to have a discussion about the whole arrangement when things have calmed down. At this point, I'm not sure this is going to work the way we hoped. And Jade...stop calling me Amby already!"

Reuben took Amber's cue and sipped the last of his tea out of his cup. "Oh yes. I have things to do this evening. Don't stress yourself too much," he said as he reached out and gently rubbed Amber's shoulder where she was smacked by her sister. "I'll be sure to text you later."

Jade watched Reuben's actions curiously, her bright eyes not missing as much as a frame of his movement. Amber inwardly groaned, but leaned into the vampire's touch, somehow sensing that he was less than pleased with the situation as well.

Reuben pulled his hand back. "It was a pleasure meeting you, Jade. I hope you have a great rest of the day." With no more ado, he smoothly exited the cafe and entered his car.

"Nice to meet you too, Reuben," Jade called after him with a grin. She watched as he left the cafe and, as soon as the door closed, rounded on Amber. "Ambyyyy, he's not just helping you with your book, is he?" Amber could feel the excitement dripping from her sister's frame and threatening to drown her in its waters.

Amber grabbed Jade by the arm and dragged her to the counter where Amber paid for her drinks with haste. Every attempt by Jade to open her mouth was met with daggers, which kept her quiet until the siblings were outside and walking down the busy street.

"Amber! That man...he's your boyfriend, isn't he?"

How her sister had jumped to that conclusion was partially a mystery, and partially a relief. Surely that meant they were doing a good job at their ruse?

But what version should she tell Jade? Her brain tore itself apart for a moment as the two sides warred with each other. If she told her they were really dating, then she would have to explain everything when they 'broke up.'

But if she told Jade the real arrangement, would she judge her sister harshly? She felt ridiculous as she ran various presentations of the plan through her head. Neither was particularly good, but the eyes burning holes in the side of her head told her she didn't have much longer to consider. "Well, kind of. We've only known each other for a few weeks, since Gabriella sent me to that speed dating thing I told you about."

"I knew it, I knew it!" Jade sang, dancing in a small circle before continuing to follow Amber down the street to Jade's car. "Didn't realize you'd go for a guy who looks like a CEO, but no judgment. Mom and Dad will be happy that you're willing to date *anyone*. Eeee! And he's so *cute* too!! How did someone like you end up with someone like *him?*"

Amber sighed and did her best not to roll her eyes. "I guess we bonded over mutually thinking the event was nonsense? And he agreed to help me with ideas for my next book, so. It has worked out so far, I guess." The starry-eyed Jade appeared content with this answer and had no further questions to ask as the pair approached Amber's apartment building.

"Is it more than one armload?" Amber asked, craning her neck to locate the items her mother had sent over. From the front seat she could see various book covers, statuettes, and collectibles peeking out of their cardboard prisons. "Did Mom decide to take everything out of my bedroom or something?" she grumbled, and received a nod in response.

Amber tossed her head back and pulled her keys out of her pocket, already beginning to wonder where she was going to stash all this stuff. "I don't have room for all this crap..."

"You could always get out of your dank and dusty low-income apartment and get something decent with more square footage. I know that you make a ton of money on book sales. There's no way you can't afford something better than this! Unless you're good at hiding a massively expensive drug habit that none of us have managed to catch onto yet." Jade's bright eyes settled teasingly on her little sister, who chuckled and shook her head.

"I'm not doing drugs, but I like this apartment. I've lived here a long time and it's comfortable. And moving sucks. And so does getting used to new surroundings."

The girls loaded up with boxes, barely getting everything inside in one trip. Jade set hers on the table, flopped onto Amber's couch, and shook her head. "You are so rigid. I only hope that this cute, well-dressed, and seemingly put-together boyfriend of yours can set you straight on a few things. Go out on a limb once in a while! Without having to be dragged there by someone else."

Her eyes flickered meaningfully at the original draft of *Under Caribbean Skies* which lay on the small table next to the couch where it had been for literal years at this point. "You might find that you *like* new surroundings. Anyway, I've got to go. Jeremy and I have to attend Todd's recital this afternoon. You *are* coming to his birthday party on the fifteenth, right? You can't let your nephew down. You're his favorite aunt, you know."

"I'm his only aunt," Amber replied cheekily, but accepted Jade's hug as she turned to head out the door.

"Doesn't matter, you're still the favorite. 6pm, my house. And bring Reuben, eh? I'm sure the family would love to meet him." She disappeared out the door and Amber was left with a sinking feeling in her gut. She'd forgotten about the celebration of her oldest nephew's eighth birthday, and she didn't particularly feel like introducing Reuben to the family right now.

Heck, she hardly felt like even talking to him.

><><>Reuben<><><

Wow. That was uncomfortable. Reuben massaged the grimace from his face as he considered how uncanny the resemblance was between Amber and her sister. Despite the bickering, she didn't seem to be a terrible person; yes, she came across as a little overprotective and maybe too excited, but seemed like a normal sister. As soon as he got home, he pulled out his phone and sent Amber a quick text.

REUBEN

> Don't let her be too hard on you. I think you look striking in your comfortable clothes. Have a great day, babe.

Okay, maybe he only added 'babe' because Amber had said he was only helping with her book. Reuben had felt an arrow pierce his chest at the introduction. He couldn't help but feel they were a little more than 'helping with my book.' He understood not coming out to her family about their arrangement; contractual relationships weren't something to brag about. But she couldn't have gone with 'friend?'

He might also have added it because it almost sounded like he was being dumped.

CHAPTER 18

><><>Mr. DeVito<><><

*I*n the days following the mess of a meeting at Tres Leches, Reuben checked his phone constantly for any sort of reply to his last message. However, nearly a week went by in complete radio silence.

And despite sending the syringe to the local crime lab for study, the police were no closer to figuring out who had sent it to Reuben. The sight of it lingered in the back of his mind, taunting him with its message. *We found you. We found you. We found you.*

He may not have known who sent it or how they found him, but their message was clear: just keeping the vampire out of politics wasn't enough for them. Instead of allowing himself to sulk, he used work as a distraction. He gave his speeches wonderfully without skipping a beat, his smile was extra broad, and he treated everyone extra kindly.

But his numbers were not changing. While they had fluctuated slightly after the press release, things stabilized in the following days. All he could think to do was throw himself harder into the various public service opportunities HOME provided.

Today's mission was a supernatural soup kitchen in the poorest part of town, where he was handing out coolers with a week's supply of blood in them. The building had once been a factory of some sort, but now stood empty aside from the two offices and large foyer used by HOME once a week.

Mr. DeVito had worked this particular location many times, and he saw many of the same faces as previous days. These people couldn't get a break! His heart contracted and his eyes stung when he stared into each familiar set of eyes. Their clothes were worn and their cheeks were gaunt, while dry tongues licked cracked lips over and over. He hoped that with each helping hand he extended that he could make their life a little better.

Many of their eyes were blood red with hunger and the vampires were anxious to get their share. Mr. DeVito watched anxiously as a few started to shove in line. He knew they would have to shut down for the day if things got out of hand, so when a small fight broke out, he didn't hesitate to throw himself between the quarreling vampires. "Please stop! There is plenty to go around!"

But the vampires didn't listen. The taller of the two, a dark-skinned man who appeared to have been turned in his forties, wrapped his large hands around the neck of the smaller vampire, another man with almond skin, bright green eyes, and the body of a twenty year old. The smaller man kicked wildly, landing a few solid blows to the other man's legs.

As he had a steady food supply, Mr. DeVito could have overpowered them. Instead, he held the two at arms length away from him and talked to them like bickering children. "Behave yourselves! You know they will close the kitchen for the day if you don't stop! There is plenty for everyone!" he pleaded, but the two men seemingly couldn't hear him.

As the vampires flailed about, Mr. DeVito felt a sudden sting on his neck as one of their hands clawed at his throat. He flinched, but didn't let go. All he wanted was to keep the situation under control. He continued holding the pair apart until he felt hands on his shoulders as other staff started to step in and put an end to the chaos. His fingers released the two men's shirts as the perpetrators were pulled apart by two hulking werewolves.

"Mr. DeVito! Let us handle this, please!"

Mr. DeVito was pulled away by security while the other two vampires were being dealt with. He backed up as requested, and in moments found himself pulled into a private office in the back of the soup kitchen. Away from the chaos of the event, Mr. DeVito sat quietly on the couch with his head pressed firmly into his hands.

He'd failed. Utterly failed. A burning mixture of anger, frustration, depression, and defeat weighed down on him and made him feel as if gravity was working extra hard to drag him to the floor.

Soon a PR representative, Evan, rushed into the office to give him a firm lecture about being a positive influence. "You know how terrible that spat is going to look on the news," the overworked werewolf sighed as Mr. DeVito's neck was patched up with a small piece of gauze and some medical tape. The wound was nothing more than a scratch, but the vampire hadn't eaten his breakfast blood bag this morning. His healing would be delayed until he was able to eat. "These types of events are supposed to boost your reputation, not ruin it!"

Despite the mess, Mr. DeVito felt like he had done nothing wrong. There was a problem and he wasn't going to let the fight escalate to ruin everyone else's week. "I couldn't let them go at each other, Evan. It's not entirely their fault. They were starving and desperate! All I wanted to do was ensure everyone got their supplies."

Evan sighed and shook his head. "But now all everyone is going to see is you in the middle of a fight, Vito. You should probably call Ms. Melburne and then go home."

The thought of calling Stella to tell her about his newest failure felt like a slap to the face. But he knew she would find out one way or another, and the best scenario for him would be heading her off at the pass with the truth instead of letting the media feed her their version.

And feed their version they did. Within an hour, every news station in the state was reporting on the fight. HOME had been trying to bring a small beacon of hope to the otherwise terrible situation the supernaturals were in, but all they managed to do was bring judgment down on their heads.

And more unfortunately, a picture spread like wildfire of Mr. DeVito holding up two grown men as if they were toddlers.

><><>Reuben<><><

"This has to stop happening." Stella pushed the newspaper across her desk and stared at Reuben. He sat slumped in the chair across from his boss, the weariness obvious in every cell of his body. He couldn't even muster up the energy to put on his Mr. DeVito facade. "Photos like this aren't going to lower the number of people actively fighting to keep you out of office."

Reuben didn't even react. His eyes remained downcast, stubbornly unfocused. Stella tapped her desk with irritation and he glanced up for a moment, but no more than that.

"Reuben," she began again in a softer tone, "there have been four more syringes delivered since we had your mail rerouted. The police have been keeping up a presence as best they can in your neighborhood, but you really need to consider our offer of a bodyguard."

He finally looked up, the fear evident in his eyes. Yet he still shook his head. "Stella, you know I can't accept. HOME already spends too much money on me. What program would we have to cut to pay for a bodyguard? Who would go hungry or homeless or jobless so I could be watched over?"

"It's an investment, Reuben. I have no doubt that every penny that HOME spends on you will be repaid in full when you get elected. But if one of those syringe-wielding maniacs hits their mark, everything we have worked for is gone. You've done enough work today. Why don't you go home and get some rest?"

He nodded and exited the building, ignoring everyone he passed on his way out. And as he pulled into his garage and the door closed securely behind him, a panic attack was already playing with the edges of his vision. His throat burned with hunger as he stumbled into the house. He barely made it to the couch before his knees gave out and he was lost to his nightmare of memories.

When he woke, he found himself kneeling by the couch with his head and arms resting on the seat cushion. The silence of late night filled his still home and rested heavier on him than the darkness, which his predator eyes could cut right through. He pulled himself up from the floor and went straight to the kitchen, barely noticing the polyfil covering the floor from a shredded pillow. His scratchy throat threatened another traumatic episode, which was the last thing he wanted right now.

Thirty seconds later his fangs punctured the soft, warm plastic of a microwaved blood bag and he sighed as the iron-laden liquid rolled down his throat. It soothed his ills, including healing the small scratch on his neck. He threw the empty packaging in the biohazard bin and returned to the couch, tugging at the tie he hadn't managed to remove before the nightmares took over.

All he wanted to do was talk to Amber.

Reuben pulled the phone out of his pocket and powered on the screen, hoping against hope that he would find a message from the only person who made him feel accepted. Well…the only person who *had* made him feel accepted. Of course he found nothing there except a notification that another meeting had been added to his schedule for tomorrow by Stella.

A new wave of depression lapped at his chest. How was he going to explain to his boss that he'd managed to screw everything up? His poll numbers were still dropping, the soup kitchen was a disaster, and Amber was still not talking to him. At this point, Reuben was starting to think they might as well give up on the election and figure out another way to get supernatural voices heard.

Yet if they did, he couldn't help feeling that there would still be a hole in his life. "I have to figure out a way to get Amber back," he murmured, leaning back against the arm of the couch and closing his eyes wearily.

"Even if it's just to be friends."

><><>Amber<><><

*A*mber couldn't concentrate and kept causing Spyro to jump off cliffs. She knew she should be working on her novel, but the last five days had only resulted in a series of depressing scenes that she couldn't bring herself to reread, much less send to Gabriella. She thought video games might help, but was proven wrong.

Every day she regretted not calling Reuben, but the more time that passed, the harder it felt. And he hadn't called her recently either. So maybe he didn't want her to call him anyway?

Today was particularly bad. But instead of letting herself freak out, she changed tactics and started cleaning. She turned on the television for some company and set about gathering up the dirty socks and abandoned t-shirts which spread across the floor like fallen autumn leaves.

Hours passed by as laundry was done, floors were scrubbed, shelves were straightened, and dust was removed. The droning sound of the TV melded into the hum of the vacuum cleaner, all meaning being lost until Amber glanced up and saw a familiar face on the screen. She immediately turned off the vacuum and dropped to the couch, eyes focused intently on the headline scrolling along the bottom of the screen.

"FIGHT BREAKS OUT AT MONSTER MEAL. ARE WE SAFE WITH THESE CREATURES ROAMING THE STREETS?"

"We are on the outskirts at a HOME-sponsored supernatural soup kitchen. A fight broke out in line as the food was being handed out, resulting in minor injuries to three vampires. If they can't get along with each other, then how are humans supposed to feel safe with them roaming the streets freely? This report is brought to you by Channel 5 news."

The more she watched, the more fury trickled into her heart. *CREATURES?* A few months ago, such a headline would barely have registered a second glance. But after getting to know Reuben...Amber tossed the remote at the TV screen and kicked the leg of the couch. These vampires were people, too! People trapped in a body they were unable to escape. Cursed with a disease they were powerless to heal and forever bound to carry.

She powered off the television as Reuben was hauled away from the fight, the crimson line on his neck all too visible. In an attempt to get the blatant hate speech out of her head, the author continued to fight dirt and grime as if they were the reporters besmirching her sort-of-boyfriend's name.

However, her attempts were thwarted by the sound of her phone ringing from its place on the couch. Amber snatched it up in case Reuben was calling, only to frown when Jade's name lit up the screen. "Hello?"

"Amber, are you dating Reuben DEVITO?? The freaking HOME rep who was in the middle of that fight today? I thought he looked familiar, but I couldn't place him until I saw him on TV. What the HELL? Aren't you afraid he's going to use you as a walking restaurant the moment you aren't looking?"

The more Jade shouted, the angrier Amber grew. She considered hanging up on her sister without saying anything, but instead she allowed her rage to find a target. "You're as bad as the rest of them, aren't you? Reuben has been nothing but polite, gentle, and sweet from the moment I met him! I thought that *you* of all people would be more accepting than that! Or do I need to remind you of Jeremy's monthly exploits?"

"My husband takes his werewolf medication and is no more dangerous than you are! There's no medication for vampirism, Amber! There's a difference between harmlessly shapeshifting once a month and being a predator." Jade's voice rose in pitch every few syllables until she was practically screaming into the phone.

Amber hung up without a further word and tossed the phone at the back of the couch, where it bounced off the cushion and came to rest on the seat. In her blind fury, she stripped off her clothing and headed for the shower. A good, long soak under scalding hot water was exactly what she needed after this afternoon. As such, she turned it up as high as she could handle and stood with the stream beating down on her head and shoulders until it melted away all the anger.

By the end, she was calm enough to pick up her phone and shoot

Jade a text. She was a bit surprised to find her sister hadn't sent *her* any while she boiled herself alive, but set it aside for the time being.

AMBER

> Sorry I lost my temper. Just please don't tell the whole family about Reuben, okay? It's still something I'm processing and I don't need to get everyone's opinions heaped on me right now.

CHAPTER 19

><><>Amber<><><

*A*mber glanced up at the clock. *Crap, I need to get moving or I'll be late to the party!* Despite feeling awkward from the fight and getting no response from her sister since yesterday, she knew things would only be worse if she skipped the family event. So she put on something a little nicer than gym shorts, grabbed her keys, and padded toward the bus stop on the corner.

In contrast to Amber's small, dark apartment, Jade's home was large and bright. Every light was on and every piece of furniture held a family member while the air hummed with conversation. Amber arrived a few minutes late and slipped into the kitchen to find out what snacks had been set out.

Jade must have accepted some of Amber's terms; nobody looked at her funny when she walked through the doors, but that didn't mean she'd been forgiven. In fact, Jade spent the first few minutes pointedly ignoring Amber's existence. She busied herself with ensuring the rest of the family was happy and comfortable, well-fed and entertained. No one seemed to notice her shunning of Amber except Amber, which suited her fine.

But she didn't go unnoticed for long. "Aunt Amby!!" screeched the trio of nieces and nephew who dropped what they were doing to hang from her gangly arms.

"Hello, munchkins," Amber replied, lifting the kids into the air and causing them to giggle. They filled her ears with the million questions of youth as she stumbled into the living room, attempting to carry the three kids still hanging from her arms and her food in her hands without spilling anything. She smiled fondly as she indulged their favorite game until she reached the couch and they scattered back to their cake.

No sooner did she sit down and shed the kids than other attention turned on her. "Hey sweetpea, Jade tells us you have an announcement to make!" Amber's elderly father, Harrison, clapped a warm and worn hand on his daughter's shoulder with a beaming smile. "She wouldn't tell us what it was, so we've all been waiting eagerly for your arrival!"

Cold horror began running through Amber's veins and she momentarily considered running out the door. But she'd already made the choice to come, and if she didn't break the news herself... Jade surely would. So she nodded to her dad and began piling the desserts on her plate into her mouth while attempting to write herself a speech.

She'd had little success by the time every eye swiveled to rest on her form, and Amber collapsed in on herself. She remained frozen for a long moment until her mother patted the seat next to her.

"Come on, Amber. Come sit here with your mama. I haven't seen you in a while!" Ivy Marcus's gentle smile managed to melt her daughter's frozen muscles and Amber hurried across the room to take the offered seat. She wrapped her warm arm around Amber's shoulder and pulled her close to her side before planting a kiss on Amber's cheek.

Safe in her mother's arms, Amber's brain rebooted. Jade shot her a look across the room which said 'hurry up or I'll tell them myself,' and Amber took a deep breath.

"I've...met someone," she said.

The room exploded into shouts of joy and questions that overlapped like the waves of the sea. Amber remained silent until everyone had calmed down somewhat and stared at her for more information. "H...His name is Reuben. We've only known each other a few weeks and have only been on a few dates, so it's nothing super intense or anything."

Again the room exploded. "TELL US ABOUT HIM!" was the most prevalent exclamation, though thankfully it was accompanied with mostly bright eyes and surprised smiles. However, Amber was unwilling to give up any more details, and eventually Ivy used her matriarch status to quiet the family.

"Now, now, everyone. Just relax. I know you're all as excited as I am, but don't overwhelm poor Amber. She'll tell us more when she's ready, won't you, dear?"

Amber nodded and with that, the ordeal was done. Her family went back to chatting animatedly amongst themselves and she began devouring the chocolate cake and lemon bars on her plate.

Surrounded by her loved ones, the author felt herself relaxing back into her normal life. Here, in this home, all the complications of her situationship could be left at the door. She felt a little bit silly for all the spinning up she had done about telling her family about Reuben, only for it to be over in less than five minutes.

That didn't stop Jade from glaring at her for not spilling *all* the beans, but both girls were sure everyone would figure it out soon enough.

Amber could feel Jade's eyes boring into the back of her head the entire evening, until everyone started going through the motions of heading home. She caught Amber at the doorway, pushed her into the foyer, and placed a hand on her shoulder.

"Amby. As your older sister, I want you to be careful. Don't let yourself be tricked by how handsome that vampire is and forget how dangerous he could be. Or ignore the possibility that he could be using you like the articles floating around the internet are saying. I don't want you to get hurt."

As much as Amber wanted to shout at her again, she'd had enough time to cool down that she could see the real concern in her sister's eyes. Jade never had anything but Amber's best interests at heart her whole life and she knew it.

"Don't worry," Amber sighed. "I don't know if we're still together anyway. I don't know if you heard me telling him the other day that we'd need to talk about things later, but...well, I kind of never responded to his messages after that." The guilt was white hot now that she had admitted to purposefully cutting Reuben out, especially after she'd been taking strides to make things real.

But Jade looked relieved. "I see. Well, perhaps it's for the best. At least he got you out of your apartment. Maybe now that you've had a taste of what dating is like, you'll be more willing to meet people. I'm sure you'll find a cute husband someday!" She wrapped her arms tightly around her little sister and pressed their foreheads together. "If I find any candidates, I'll send them your way."

Amber blushed and struggled out of Jade's arms, causing her to laugh brightly. "We'll see how that goes," she responded before giving her sister another hug and disappearing into the night.

CHAPTER 20

>‹›‹›Reuben‹›‹›‹

*R*euben couldn't take it any longer. It had been a full week and he was tired of dodging Stella's questions about his next date and worrying about the status of his relationship. If Amber wasn't going to call him, he would call *her*. She may not have a hard deadline on her novel, but if he needed to move on to Plan B? He needed to know *now*. Not to mention, he missed her. Badly.

As tempting as it was to just text, Reuben knew this wasn't exactly a texting-type conversation. And so he tapped Amber's contact and held the phone to his ear. With each ring his planned script changed, right up until her voicemail message began to play.

Nope. That was not going to do. If he knew anything about Amber by this point, it was that the likelihood of her actually being busy right now was incredibly low. So rather than leaving a message, Reuben hit redial. And redial. And redial. "Stop ignoring me!" he grumbled as the fourth attempt rang and rang.

And finally, Amber picked up.

"Oh thank the gods," Reuben breathed, every one of his speeches immediately flying out the window. "Amber, I am so sorry. I've been an idiot."

"Yes. Yes you have," came the reply. Amber's voice sounded rather cold and Reuben felt his heart sink. "But...so have I. I'm sorry, too. I definitely overreacted the other day. It was just too much too fast, and I needed some time to process. And then it felt more and more awkward to call so I just didn't."

The sheer amount of relief that washed over Reuben threatened to drown him. He had to clear his throat a couple of times before he could get any words out. "I was waiting to hear from you every day," he admitted, not caring if he sounded desperate. "I missed you so much."

"I missed you, too. I'm glad you called. Even if I ignored you three times."

They both began to laugh, and Reuben felt the tension in his muscles melt away. "So...before the whole cafe debacle, you said you'd be willing to come over to my place. Is that still on the table? Because I would love to have you over for a quiet movie night to make up for all the public nonsense."

There was a slight pause on the other end of the phone. Reuben's shoulders tightened again, but finally Amber replied, "Sure. How about tonight?"

><><>Amber<><><

The eight hours between Reuben inviting her over and the agreed meeting time had been torture. Amber hurriedly opened her ride share app, entered the address Reuben provided, and glanced at herself in the mirror. Would her baggy pajama pants and oversized band tee be acceptable for spending time with a politician? Would Reuben think she wasn't taking this seriously enough?

In the end, she decided she didn't care and simply slipped her wallet into the pocket of her cotton pants. The driver arrived minutes later and Amber climbed into the car, a mixture of nerves, curiosity, and excitement rushing through her veins.

It was a moderate distance between their homes; usually in a car ride of this length, Amber would have fallen asleep. However, she was too worked up to even close her eyes this time. The city rolled by in streetlight-illuminated normality outside the car windows and she daydreamed about who might be behind the building walls. Normal humans? Vampires? Werewolves?

It was interesting to think that from the outside, there was no way to know. Nor did it matter. The apartments could contain anyone, but they were all equally peaceful in the nighttime quiet. If only other people could see that!

The car drove up to a gated community and, after confirmation that Amber was on the guest list, the gate opened. They pulled up in front of the unit Reuben had indicated and Amber stepped out of the car, thanked the driver, and strolled up to the door. She hesitated a moment with her knuckles hovering over the wood before she worked up the courage to knock three times.

The neighborhood was much, much fancier than her own. Not that she didn't like her neighborhood; well, her apartment at least. There were constantly sirens outside her building reminding her that she never left the sketchy building she'd moved into for college, but hey. It was home. She heard a sound behind the door, the lock disengaging, and squashed the obnoxious voice in her mind which told her she was probably at the incorrect address.

><><>Reuben<><><

*R*euben provided his address to Amber the moment she asked to make good on the movie night rain check, despite needing to finish his workday first. While he probably could have waited until the next day, he'd missed Amber and insisted they meet up that night. And besides, the gated community in which he lived was quite effective at keeping unwanted guests out. If this second attempt at a relationship went south, he could take Amber off the visitor list.

He didn't really need to tidy up much, either. The few glasses he'd left in the sink went into the dishwasher and a quick vacuum removed the dust which had settled in while he'd been too depressed to care. Reuben glanced into the fridge and pantry, finding he had plenty of drinks...but only an open box of microwave popcorn for snacks. "I should have picked up some human food before I drove home," he mumbled. "I don't want to be a bad host..."

Dressed in a pink Nike shirt and black joggers, Reuben began preparing the upstairs living room for their movie night while he waited for Amber to arrive. His windows were tinted, but he still pulled the thick curtains shut to give them full privacy. He placed two folded quilts on the large, L-shaped couch and turned on the flat screen which was hanging on the wall.

The five battle-ready replica lightsabers hanging on the wall and tall, dark bookshelves received a quick dusting as well. Said shelves were lined with mostly romance novels sorted by the author's last name. A few spots were empty; their occupants made their home on the coffee table for the time being. *Beneath Caribbean Skies* by Henry Allan Spencer graced the top of the stack. It was well-worn and had been read repeatedly.

By the time Reuben was done preparing the living room for their date, he heard footsteps approaching his front door. They paused for a moment before a soft knock rapped against the wood. With a grin, Reuben flashed down the stairs and answered the call.

Amber's hand was still in a knocking position as the sturdy door was opened. "Gem, it's so good to see you again." Reuben took a step back and motioned for his maybe girlfriend to come inside. His eyes glanced at his guest's attire, and he approved. This was a comfy movie date night and Amber passed the vibe check.

"Please come in," Reuben exclaimed with a big grin tugging at the corner of his mouth, despite his attempt at calming his excitement. He couldn't believe Amber was in his house. And that she had finally contacted him again. This was one of the only places Reuben could be himself and he was glad he could share it with someone important.

By the front door, there was a little black rug for shoes and hooks on the wall for jackets. Most of the rest of the walls were bare. His way of decorating was unique, to say the least. Random pieces that only he could consider art sat on end tables and a single plant sat on the kitchen counter next to a sizable bowl of assorted candies. Books, glazed clay pots, old records and movie memorabilia were scattered around the house.

Amber smiled at the nickname and stepped inside, removing her shoes and stepping with her stocking feet onto the soft carpet of the rug before following Reuben deeper into the home. As soon as the door closed, she pushed her luck and wrapped her arms around Reuben's neck. She kissed him softly on the cheek before letting go and taking a step back. "It's so nice to see you again."

With the warmth of Amber's lips still lingering on his cheek, Reuben allowed his grin to widen. "So, this is my house... HOME built it and allowed me to live here. Whether it was to keep me protected from death threats or keep the media away from my windows, I don't know, but I appreciate the privacy nonetheless."

Reuben walked up a few stairs, looking back to watch Amber checking out his house. Surprisingly, he cared about what Amber thought. A lot. "I can give you a quick tour if you'd like or we can save that for another day. The best part is my living room."

Amber's eyes scanned every visible surface and she smiled at the subtle nods to nerd-dom which were sprinkled here and there. "I guess tours are most logical for a first visit. But we can do that later, if you want. HOME didn't spare any expense, did they?"

"They definitely treat me well. I think it's mostly so they can test models of products that will go into future supernatural-friendly households, though. They wanted to make sure their products would be useful, and I was their guinea pig. The tinted windows, for example. The organization had to make sure it would block out enough sunlight during the day while still maintaining a somewhat normal appearance on the outside. They work wonderfully after a few failed attempts."

Amber nodded and followed Reuben up the stairs. "This is like, the ritzy part of town, too," she said. "Maybe someday I'll move out of my little apartment and into something half this nice. I think you'd be mortified by the amount of stuff I have covering my walls..."

Reuben shook his head. "Oh, I don't think it will bother me. I'm just not a great decorator. I buy things that look cool that I can touch or use." As he entered the living room, Reuben spoke again. "I didn't plan that far ahead, but I have microwaveable popcorn and hard candies for food. However, I do have a bunch of drinks. Juice, beer, wine, soda, Capri Suns... if you get hungry, I can order a pizza or some Chinese food."

The sweet scent of vanilla drifted through the air as Reuben listed the food and drink options; Amber listened to this part with rapt attention. "Capri Suns are like...my favorite thing. I don't care that they are for children. There's something amusing to me about stabbing the little pouches with a straw.

"And I'm not really an alcohol person, but juice and I are best friends. And orange soda. And Chinese food, the crappier the better. It's like you've already found the road map to my heart. Not that it's that hard."

Reuben laughed and held out his hands, spinning in a slow circle to show off the living room. "It's not much, but it's my little comfort zone. Soft couch, books, this huge TV... well, huge from when I was a kid. These things can hang on walls, now." He chuckled as he thought back to the black and white or box TVs that he grew up seeing.

Amber stood on her tiptoes and leaned over the couch to get a closer look before getting distracted again by the sheer number of books in the room. And the TV which wasn't from 2005. "Yeah, I've seen like, 120 inch TVs. Who needs that? At that point, you might as well set up a movie theater in your house and charge admission."

Amber's eyes widened at the light sabers. "Are these the battle-ready kind?!" she exclaimed, seeming to teleport over to the couch to stare at the shiny objects. Her hand reached out for them automatically, but she quickly regained her control and sucked it back to her side. "Can...I mean, do you mind if I examine them more closely?"

Reuben nodded. "We can play with them if you want! Nobody has been willing to before." He then motioned to his wall of books. "And this is what I think you'll like the most. I have a bunch of books; I like keeping basically every book I read. Plus, cracking open a new print is a guilty pleasure of mine. The crisp smell of fresh ink and paper tickles the brain perfectly."

"There's something amazing about new book smell," she agreed. "Though old book smell is just as intoxicating." She moved to another bookshelf then another, until she'd made a full circle and found herself standing in front of the coffee table.

She stared at the intimately familiar cover of the first book on the stack. The color immediately drained from her face and her eyes widened like a deer faced with oncoming traffic. "Oh, you read Henry Allan Spencer? How do you feel about his book?" Amber managed, somehow, to eke out in a casual and definitely-not-panicked tone. She sat down on the couch and picked up the book, running her hand over the cover for a moment before setting it back down. "Have you finished it yet? If so, how did you feel about the ending?"

Reuben followed Amber over to the couch and plopped down next to her. "Oh? *Beneath Caribbean Skies*? Yeah. The ending is great. He's a fantastic writer. Somehow, Spencer knows the right words to use at the right times. He really believes in the romance of the story instead of popping out another bland replica novel. Too bad he's only released one book. I always felt like he could have done a sequel if he wanted, but maybe that's where the story needed to end. It could be me craving more."

Reuben pointed at the book and flicked his finger up, as if telling Amber to take it. "I've read this one at least a dozen times while keeping my eye out in case he ever releases another book. Do you want to read it? You can borrow it if you want. I would like it back when you're finished, though. I'll definitely read it again."

"Oh, I have more than one copy already, thanks though. I'm so glad you liked the ending, too. I felt like they'd established enough of a foundation before they became a couple that it would be believable. Romances are more impactful when they're capable of being real, don't you think?"

Amber's eyes got a faraway look in them and she sat on the arm of the couch. "Yes, most of them are an exaggerated and unlikely scenario, but I don't feel like I can get into the story when I don't believe it could happen in a perfect world." She sighed and blushed at Reuben's touch and the high praise. "I've read it far more times than I would be willing to admit, even if I had kept track."

It didn't seem odd to Reuben that Amber owned multiple copies of such a good book. Hardcover, paperback, special editions…they were all worth something to someone who loved the tale within the pages. But he froze for a moment as Amber's words struck a chord.

Romances are more impactful when they're capable of being real.

Reuben felt those words applied both to the novel and to his girl-friend arrangement. The harder they tried to make the relationship look real, the more impactful it would be. Reuben knew he'd be simmering over that phrase for quite some time.

But rather than sit in awkward silence, Reuben jumped into host mode. "How about I go get some takeout menus and a juice or two for you? And I can order whatever you like." Money wasn't an issue as long as it made Amber happy. He didn't think of it as a waste, nor did he intend on asking for it back. A little cash was a small sacrifice to keep his human companion comfortable.

Just as Reuben was about to flash down the stairs, he froze. He had shown off his speed to Amber before, but the usage of his powers was usually less filtered in his own home. "Um…I'm sorry, I never asked if flashing makes you uncomfortable. Are you okay with it? It might be disorienting or disturbing to some people." He knew that Amber wanted to live the experience of dating a vampire for her book, but knowing and seeing it happen were different things.

Amber had settled against the arm of the couch and curled her feet up next to herself comfortably, draping the blanket over her legs. A surprised look colored her features. "I don't mind at all. You be you, Benji. Flash away! As in, around your house. Moving at high speed. Not like…flash in the other meaning. Because I know that's what you didn't mean. I don't need to see anything like that yet."

Amber pulled the blanket up over her head for a moment as her face burned. "I'll hang out here for the next point five seconds."

The smile on Reuben's face widened at Amber's poor choice of words and stumbled recovery. He couldn't resist; he had to say something. "Aww babe, if you want me to take my pants off, all you'd have to do is ask." His tone was simultaneously flirtatious and teasing, but meant as a joke.

There wasn't much time for Amber to wallow. "I think we're

firmly in 'pants on' territory still," she giggled from beneath the blanket.

Not that Reuben heard her. He was gone only two seconds before he set a handful of cold drink pouches on the table and handed over the menu for his favorite Chinese place. "You can order anything you want. Don't worry about the price or anything. I've got it."

Amber pulled down the blanket and examined the menu. After an awkward amount of time, she settled on something safe. "How about orange chicken, chow mein, and egg rolls? Is there anything you like in particular? Though I guess you can order for yourself without having to tell me the order first."

She laughed at herself and handed Reuben the menu, holding out one arm so he could tuck himself into her side while he ordered. Reuben plopped himself into the indicated place, originally leaving two or three inches between their thighs. However, he ended up snuggling under Amber's arm only moments later. "I can't eat a lot, so I stick to the soup." He pulled his phone out of his pocket and opened the Wok In app.

It suggested his usual order, a container of easily-digestible chicken mushroom soup, but he swiped it away, choosing instead to call the store. "Hello. Ah, yes, hello Wendy! It's me."

The excited voice on the other end of the phone caused Reuben to chuckle. He loved this family-owned restaurant, especially because they never treated him poorly for being a vampire. "I would like to place an order for delivery, please. Oh, yes, the usual would be fine. But can I also add orange chicken, chow mein, and a side of egg rolls?"

There was a few seconds' pause before Reuben spoke again. "You know, can you double that order and bag it separately for my gatekeeper? Yes please. Thank you. Yes, you too. Have a great night." Reuben placed his phone on the table, as if showing it would not be a distraction.

Amber stretched a little to wiggle into a more comfortable position and spoke. "You must really like your gatekeeper to order him dinner, too."

"Oh, that. I have my food dropped off at the gate and he keeps it safe until I come pick it up. It's only fair to feed him after taunting him with food while he keeps the neighborhood safe." With food taken care of, his mind flipped to the next order of business. Though both parties had done their best to shove the elephant out of the room, they needed to discuss the last week.

Rather than continuing to hope Amber would bring it up, Reuben cut his misery short. "I am glad that you answered the phone." He buried his face in Amber's curls, savoring the warmth and scent he'd grown so fond of. "And not because I was worried about the election. After a week apart, I realized how much I'd already grown used to your presence in my life. It was lonely when I couldn't call or text you to talk about my day."

"I am sorry that I ghosted you. I let my fear get in the way of what I now know I wanted." Amber took the vampire's hand into her own and began massaging the palm in slow circles. "But...do you really forgive me?"

Reuben pulled his head back enough that he could make direct contact with Amber's large, pleading eyes. "Of course I do, Gem. And I also believe we have both learned everything we could from the experience, so we should leave it in the past. What do you think?" He ran his free hand through Amber's hair and down the side of her neck to settle on her shoulder.

That sounded wonderful.

CHAPTER 21

><><>**Amber**<><><

*E*ager to put the unpleasantness in the past where it belonged, Amber changed the subject again. "So, did you have a movie picked out? I picked the last one, so it's your turn. I'm happy with just about anything. There's a lot to be learned about someone by the movies they choose, you know. Same with the books they read. And you," she looked around at all the books again, "give off the vibe of a man with good taste. If I do say so myself."

A cheeky grin crossed Amber's face and she rested her chin on Reuben's head, enjoying the softness of his hair. She wrapped her arms around him and gave him a squeeze. Warmth spread from her spine to her fingertips in a pleasant, tingling sensation.

"Well, I appreciate the compliment, but wait until you hear my movie choices. You might bail on me. I had either *Star Wars: Revenge of the Sith* or *The Proposal* with Sandra Bullock in mind. Opposite ends of the spectrum, but both are great options. Feel free to say no." Reuben leaned into the hug as his stuck hand squeezed Amber's knee. He would have returned the hug if he weren't at such a weird angle from cuddling.

Amber looked up and spotted the light sabers again, reached up, and retrieved one. She ran her fingers over the metal grip and solid blade, admiring the quality. "I've never had one of these fancy sabers. Once I had one of the cheap collapsible plastic ones, but I have no idea what happened to it.

"It doesn't really make sense to choose a movie before the food gets here because we'll be interrupted. Why don't we have a little test of these beauties while we wait and then I can decide?" She jumped up and stood on the couch, looking for all the world like a grown-up child in her baggy pajamas and beaming grin.

"Mhm. Those collapsible ones were exactly why I had to get these. One good smack with the plastic ones and they would break." Reuben reached up as well, grabbing Emperor Palpatine's replica saber. The handle was gold and chrome and the saber was red. His thumb traced the power button, pressing to light the blade. The handle also made noise as it lit up, almost like the real deal.

Reuben jumped away from the couch and grabbed the TV remote. He opened YouTube and pulled up the music for Obi-Wan and Anakin's fight, then turned around with a smirk as he held his saber at the ready. "Come to the daaark side!" he rumbled, attempting to sound like Palpatine as the orchestral music played in the background. He smirked as they began dancing around his living room.

With lightsaber in hand, Amber knew there was only one answer. "Do you really think you can bring back the Sith?!" she exclaimed, jumping down from the couch and putting in her first swing. She missed, because she was the least sporty human being known to mankind. But that didn't stop her from dramatically cackling and flipping around for another swing. Once in a while her strikes were true, and once in a while she managed to block Reuben's.

Reuben might have had super speed, but it was much more fun playing with Amber properly. The sabers tapped together on multiple occasions, both handles bursting to life with battle sounds. As far as Amber could tell, Reuben was having the time of his life.

"I'm already on the dark side!" Amber called, lost enough in her roleplay that she didn't notice that she was getting dangerously close to the real enemy: the coffee table. One more step back and she found herself stopped suddenly. Well, her feet were. Her top half kept its momentum and she tumbled toward the wooden menace.

Without thinking, Reuben flashed to save her. Amber reflexively closed her eyes and tensed her muscles for impact, only to find herself cradled in Reuben's soft embrace rather than laying across the table-top. His arm wrapped up Amber's back to her neck, cradling her softly. His other hand gripped the edge of the couch while his legs were on either side of her hips.

Any physical space that could have been between them was gone. At first Reuben was frozen, but he slowly began to move to check on her. "Gem. Are you okay? I should have moved that table..."

Slowly Amber's eyes opened and she found herself face-to-face with Reuben, their noses mere centimeters apart. "I'm fine," she whispered, her breath hot on Reuben's face. "Though this is one of the most stereotypical romance novel situations I've ever been in." She did her best to help Reuben get them both standing and made no move to escape his embrace when they were steady.

Steady, until Reuben pressed his lips to her forehead, and Amber's legs turned to jelly. Amber hadn't hit her head, but any pain disappeared after the magic cure.

"Muwah. All better." Reuben loosened his grip until their only point of contact was his hand on Amber's lower back, in case she hadn't quite gotten her balance yet. It was a good thing Reuben kept his hand there, or Amber certainly would have toppled over.

"You sure you're okay?" Reuben checked over Amber tenderly.

Instead of stepping away, Amber leaned against Reuben's hand and nodded. "Yes, I'm fine. And your table is fine too." That usual cheeky grin covered her face, but her eyes were more intensely focused on the vampire's face than ever before.

She felt something stirring deep in her heart, something she'd never truly experienced before. Amber thought she knew a little something about love; in fact, she might have said she was a bit of an expert. An expert in describing it. Thinking about it. Writing about it. But as she stared into those intense and worried eyes, suddenly Amber realized she had never known a single thing about love.

It was a terrifying prospect. Suddenly the pair of them were standing at the edge of a high cliff, one step away from falling off completely into an unknown space. It was terrifying, exhilarating, and mysterious all wrapped up in one package.

Amber found herself leaning closer to that perfect face. Her arms wrapped around Reuben's shoulders and hands worked their way into his hair, tangling themselves in his soft waves. Closer and closer their lips came until mere millimeters away when Amber paused. Did she dare? This close, her entire world became vanilla and sandalwood, snowy skin and jet-black hair.

Her heart pounded in her ears as she stared into Reuben's gold-flecked eyes. Her lungs seemed to forget how to open, holding her breath hostage. Her eyes traced his sharp nose and his perfect eyebrows. His lips were vibrantly red against a backdrop of expansive clouds. Was it her imagination, or were they slightly pursed?

Screw it, she thought, but before she could move, Reuben took the dive and closed the gap. He placed a tender kiss on Amber's lips, his hands gripping her band shirt and tugging it toward him.

How many stereotypical things could she have written about the moment those chilled, pillowy lips sought hers and held on for dear life? Zero, because her brain simply short-circuited. Her fingers entrenched themselves in his hair and her body arched toward him, seeking his form.

His hands slid down her shoulder blades and settled on her hip bones, sending a feeling of frosty autumn deep into her core. He pulled her closer and she made no move to resist, instead seeking more. More closeness. More of his teeth running along her bottom lip.

Truth be told, Amber had never kissed anyone, much less a vampire. She wasn't sure what she should have been expecting, but Reuben's strong grip and marble lips had caught her off guard. Waves of hormones drowned her brain in a pleasant buzz of natural intoxication.

The pair lingered there for a long moment until Amber had to breathe. She pulled back and was tempted to go for a second or third kiss, but instead rested her forehead on Reuben's before anything more serious could happen.

Her legs felt a bit unstable and she clung to Reuben to avoid falling over. Was kissing always like this? Because if so, she had *really* wasted far too much time finding out. She finally found her breath as the vampire pulled away and her eyes opened.

"I don't care about the table...not the way I'm starting to care about you, Amber." Reuben's voice was smoky and wobbly all at once; the kiss had obviously affected him.

Caring about her? What did he mean by that? Amber's jaw fell open to question his meaning when a disembodied voice broke the moment.

"Your delivery has arrived at the gate, Mr. DeVito."

Conflicting emotions swirled in Amber's heart and she gave Reuben a squeeze before breaking their embrace and pivoting to sit down on the couch.

Reuben let out a shaky breath. "Curse that intercom! I don't want the food getting cold, but I'll have to walk at a normal speed. I don't want to freak out the neighbors." His voice was still low and he sounded a bit disappointed that the food had arrived so soon. That's what he got for being a favorite regular at the Wok In...

"Okay, I'll wait right here. That way we won't get distracted on the way and make the walk take longer." She gave Reuben a smile that didn't match the turmoil in her stomach and wrapped the blanket around herself protectively. "I'll be ready for food when you get back!"

Really, Amber also needed a few minutes to process what had just happened. Her brain was a muddle of hormones giving conflicting signals. As soon as Reuben was out of sight, Amber relaxed and stared off into space.

What a strange night this was shaping up to be! She'd had her first kiss, an event she'd always imagined would be nothing but pure bliss. And it was! Yet Jade's words echoed in her mind, reminding her that she was putting himself in danger by spending time alone with a predator.

Guilt took over in a heartbeat. Reuben wasn't a monster! He was handsome, kind, polite, and gentle. After all the times Amber had insisted Reuben was another human with an incurable condition, how could she be thinking such awful thoughts? Besides, they'd spent plenty of time together. If he was going to hurt Amber, surely there would have been signs by now, right? Taking hold of that thought, Amber loosened the blanket and allowed herself to breathe more freely.

That left one more sticking point. Reuben said he *cared* about her. Granted, he compared it to caring for a table so perhaps he meant he felt like they were becoming actual friends? That would be easier to believe if he hadn't taken the offer of a kiss moments before saying it. And his voice didn't sound like someone telling a friend they were fond of them, right?

Amber kicked herself for not saying anything in response. "Pathetic loser," she grumbled, punching herself in the head. "How did you manage to get yourself into this situation? You've gotten yourself tangled up in a messy relationship and allowed yourself to start getting feelings for this guy! You even gave him your first kiss! Idiot!"

She let out a loud groan and flopped back against the couch. Was it going to be super awkward when Reuben returned with their food? Or could Amber possibly play it off like nothing had happened?

Rather than allow herself to make the decision, Amber figured she would take Reuben's lead. Surely Reuben had kissed someone before? He would know the usual protocol for these kinds of things. By the time she heard the sound of the door opening downstairs and Reuben's footsteps, the author had talked herself into a quiet corner of her mind. Everything would be fine!

><><>**Reuben**<><><

The last thing Reuben wanted to do was leave Amber after something as confusing as their first kiss, but maybe a walk in the chilled night air would do him good. It might organize his thoughts so he could understand what was happening.

Reuben slipped on a pair of tennis shoes and walked out into the night. It wasn't that far to the gatehouse, only a few houses down and to the left, but it felt like an eternity. Each step contained a desperate prayer that he wouldn't come home to an empty couch and Amber climbing the back fence.

He ran his fingers through his messy hair, every vulgarity that he knew running on a track in his mind. *I screwed everything up. I kissed her. This was a business transaction, and my sappy self* KISSED HER. *Why am I like this with her?!*

Why he caught her was obvious; he knew how fragile humans could be compared to vampires. But more importantly, he felt protective of her. He didn't know where the feeling came from or when he started to feel that way. Maybe the bullet they dodged with the article unlocked a new level in Reuben's brain, or the solitude of their week apart. There was a line, but Reuben couldn't see it as the boundary completely blurred between partner and *partner.*

He had gotten so caught up trying to be a perfect boyfriend that he forgot to check his emotions at the door. This was no longer just a business arrangement. He should have been keeping better track about what he actually felt for Amber.

And he knew why he'd kissed those soft, warm lips. It had been almost two months now since the deep silence and proximity in the aquarium had tempted him, and they were only holding hands at that point. Tonight Amber had to wrap her arms around his neck and tangle her fingers in his hair...a pleased shiver passed through his core at the memory as his hand instinctively rubbed the back of his head where Amber's hand had been.

He could feel the warm breath against his lips once more, so close a sheet of paper may not have fit between them. He shook his head, trying to get rid of the phantom sensation. This was supposed to be temporary. There weren't supposed to be messy emotions involved.

All too soon and all too slowly, Reuben arrived at the guard booth to retrieve the food. Like usual, Reuben took one bag and was about to take the other, but turned back with a glimmer in his eyes. He offered the second to the guard, whose face lit up with a huge smile.

"Maaan! Mr. DeVito, sir, thank you! My stomach was growling just smelling your dinner!"

Reuben's lips turned up into a soft smile without teeth. "Of course. Thank you for working so hard. I appreciate it. Have a great shift." He then stepped away from the guard booth and hurried home to his guest.

CHAPTER 22

><><>**Amber**<><><

The glorious scent of grease-laden Chinese food filled the air, heralding the arrival of dinner. "Mmm, look at that delicious snack," Amber teased, choosing bravado to hide her previously conflicted feelings. "The food looks good, too." She accepted the boxes of food and scooted against the arm of the couch to make sure there was plenty of room for both of them to use the coffee table. The coffee table, which was the instigator of the whole confusing mess.

Amber took her boxes out of the bag and Reuben grabbed his container of mushroom soup and a black plastic spoon. She opened up the noodles, breathed in appreciatively, and plunged her plastic fork into the soy sauce-flavored goodness.

"You sure sounded convincing in the press release, by the way. If I didn't know better, I would think you were telling the truth up there," Amber said, then filled her mouth with noodles. A few too many noodles, it turned out, as she looked up at Reuben with large eyes and noodles hanging out of her lips.

It was quite comical; Amber did her best to chew quickly and pull the stragglers in, but Reuben had plenty of time to see her chipmunk-cheeks-and-squiggly-noodles face. He also had plenty of time to reply while her mouth was conveniently busy.

Reuben's armor cracked and he chuckled, "Good, huh? They always do a great job. I hope you enjoy it. And you didn't have to watch that boring thing..." He set his soup down on the table and carefully played with the mushrooms floating in the broth to busy his hands. "Thank you, though. I do appreciate it. I have a very skilled team backing me up to help write my speeches so I don't look like a fool to the public."

Amber shrugged and pulled the last of the noodles into her mouth. Once she swallowed them, she smiled and shook her head. "I did need to! Had to make sure you announced us properly, didn't I?" Her voice was cheeky and she managed a small laugh. "And I rather wanted to see your face. It's rather pleasant to look at, you know. Does that make me a creepy stalker girlfriend?"

Another laugh filled her nostrils and Amber took a second bite of noodles, a smaller one this time. "I don't know why I've never tried this place before. I'll have to go there again."

"It's only creepy if you start cutting out newspaper articles and putting them on the wall. I appreciate it nonetheless and I also love looking at your beautiful face." Reuben reached for Amber's hand and carefully laced their fingers together, allowing them to rest their hands on the couch. "Hey. I know you said that dating wasn't something you've done before... but have you ever wanted to? I mean..."

He took a deep breath between his thoughts, met Amber's gaze, and continued, "You write about romance and create love stories. Did you ever want your own story? Have you ever imagined finding a special person and having an extravagant wedding? You know... settling down and maybe buying a cat or dog? The white picket fence life?"

Amber thought quietly, not entirely sure how to answer. She'd never really considered that she might end up alone. Perhaps it was her constant stream of romantic scenarios that gave her that feeling, but she'd always imagined that someday she'd be swept off her feet and live happily ever after.

"I've never really been against it," she finally started, shifting slightly so she could look Reuben in the eye, "but the last time I allowed myself to actually like someone, they ended up stalking me for over a year, breaking into my bedroom, and stabbing me." Amber lifted her shirt a few inches to reveal the pink, raised flesh of a long-healed knife wound in her side just below her ribs.

Reuben grew solemn, his eyes darkening. "And that's why you are so concerned about publicity, isn't it? You don't want him to find you."

Amber's eyes shimmered and she nodded. "Yeah. He still doesn't even have his first parole hearing for another year, but even after all these years...I still have nightmares about that night. About feeling like I was being hunted. I never thought something like that could come from just innocently chatting with someone online. Never thought he'd be someone entirely different than the man who told me he loved me and wanted to marry me when I turned 18."

A curse whistled through Reuben's teeth. "Oh, Gem...I feel like the world's biggest jerk for not taking your concerns as seriously as I should. I totally understand why you were so upset and ghosted me, now. I'm so sorry."

"It's fine."

"No, it's not *fine*." Reuben reached out and took Amber's hand, raising it to lift her chin. "It was insensitive of me to not even ask why you were so afraid. But I swear this to you: No harm will come to you on my account. If I have to abuse my power as a politician to make sure that scumbag never gets paroled, I will do it."

And Amber could tell by the fire in his eyes and words that he *meant* it. She shivered and decided to change the topic. "What about you, Benji?" she asked instead. "You've got a pretty good life, as far as I can tell. But have you considered getting a real partner? You've been far and above what I ever imagined to be the perfect boyfriend. You've spoiled me for anybody else at this point."

She didn't know what answer she hoped Reuben would give. Well, somewhere inside she hoped that he would say something that would clue Amber in on his real feelings. Surely Reuben wouldn't have gotten so excited during the kissing if he didn't feel anything for her, right? There was no denying what *she'd* felt in that short experiment.

But was that the excitement of physical contact, or was it the person she was kissing?

Reuben propped himself on his elbow. "I appreciate the compliments, but…" He dragged out the pause, trying to procrastinate the admission dancing on the tip of his tongue. "My job, especially when rising through the ranks to where I am now, has required most of my time. It doesn't have a great home and work life balance, like I warned you when we met."

He sighed softly and rested his jaw on the arm holding him up. "I haven't had the best of luck with partners, either. I've told you about the ones that did it for money or ten seconds in the spotlight, but I don't think I've mentioned the assassination attempt."

Amber stiffened and her wide eyes turned on the vampire. "Assassination attempt? You really *have* had bad luck with relationships, too. Or perhaps your taste in women is just poor…I mean, look at the slob you're dating now. That chick is a *loser.*" She looked down at herself and giggled, knowing she was only trying to ignore her own demons.

Somehow, he also chuckled at the memory. "Are you questioning my judgment?! My girlfriend is the opposite of a loser!" he teased and tapped Amber's nose. "It's fine. I'm fine. He had strong views on the integration of supernaturals, and they were the opposite of mine. I don't think he ever actually loved me anyway."

He paused again, his voice lowering and the chuckles subsiding. "I guess when I was a teen, I imagined moving out, going to college, and finding a really hot spouse. I never told my parents that I was bisexual, but that didn't matter. My brother accidentally let it slip about my first boyfriend and my father immediately disowned me. My mother always followed my father, and that was that. It wasn't long after that that I had my run-in with a vampire.

"I guess I never thought much of truly settling down after that. I knew my life was different and with my extended lifespan…I guess I'm afraid to lose that special someone I made a life with. And I swore the moment that vampire's fangs broke my skin that I would never do that to someone I loved."

Reuben hugged Amber a little tighter. "Having someone to enjoy life with doesn't sound terrible, though. I've been enjoying the time

I've spent with you. I wanted to ditch work for you *and I'm a workaholic.*"

Amber hugged Reuben back and ran her fingers through the vampire's dark hair. "I can't believe your family was willing to disown you over something so stupid. It's not like you chose this life, you know? Mine will probably have a lot to say about it once it sinks in, but I can't imagine they'll do anything that drastic. Just, uh. Sounds like I won't be meeting the in-laws any time soon." It was a poor attempt at a joke, but the author hoped that it would lighten the mood a little.

"For the time being, I will happily spoil you, Gem. I don't know how you remained single for so long. Beautiful, intelligent, a little nerdy with delicious lips? *You* are girlfriend material." He ran his finger along Amber's jaw and pressed it to her lips.

A tingle followed Reuben's finger and Amber felt a shiver like static in her spine. "If someone like *me* is girlfriend material, then someone like *you* is definitely husband material. Just saying," she insisted. "I'm sorry if this question is totally offensive, but...if you're afraid of losing the one you've built a life with, have you considered maybe there's another vampire out there for you? I mean, I know the human population is still much, much larger than the supernatural one, but I can't imagine that no other vampire wants my hot, sweet, funny, kind, lovable, amazing boyfriend for their own."

"It sounds a lot easier than it is..." he mumbled.

Amber paused for a moment, deciding if she really wanted to admit what she was feeling. She didn't wait long before saying, "I guess it doesn't matter. Now they'd have to fight me for him. Because apparently I'm more than a little bit possessive."

She gave Reuben the hardest hug she could manage, marveling how someone whose skin felt like fine marble could still be so soft and lovely to hug. "I wouldn't mind if you ditched work to spend time with me, though. You need it."

"I suppose so." Reuben pointed the remote at the TV and pressed play, filling the room with the opening music of *Star Wars* and effectively cutting off the conversation.

Amber frowned, but Reuben had made such an obvious statement with the action that she didn't dare continue that thread. Instead she picked up her orange chicken and began shoveling it into her mouth in an attempt to soothe her irritation.

"I didn't ask your permission before…" Reuben's voice cut through the chilly silence that had settled into the space between the pair and caught Amber off guard. She turned her head and he clarified, "I should have asked before, you know…kissing you. But I'm not sorry I did it. And I'm surprised you don't have much experience in the dating field. You're a great kisser."

Amber paused, taking a couple of deep breaths while she made her decision and the pieces fell into place. She reached out and pulled Reuben into her embrace. Wrapping her arms around his torso, Amber rested her chin on the vampire's shoulder and tenderly pressed her lips to his neck.

"I gave you permission when I almost went for it myself," she whispered, her breath hot on his neck. She wrapped her small, warm hands around his large, chilled ones and gave them a squeeze. "You did nothing wrong. But I'm glad I performed satisfactorily. I have to admit…that was my first kiss. I have no regrets saving it for you."

She kissed Reuben's jaw this time and pulled him closer, draping her leg over top of his lap as she settled into a position where Reuben lay against her. Perhaps she was pushing her luck, but it was a push she was happy to make.

If they were going to act like a couple in public, it would be best to find their limits in private first, right? And besides. She was supposed to be writing a convincing romance novel. And convincing romance novels included convincing intimacy.

Reuben didn't resist the tug. "Your first? I would have made it a little more romantic if I had known. Like a scene out of the movies." Emboldened by the positive response to his apology, he went a little further. "I'm not expecting an answer right away, but if you wanted to, or if you didn't mind, or…if you would be okay with casual kissing in public, it might help convince people we're really dating. And give you more imperial information for your book. Only if you are comfortable with it. And aren't turned off by kissing, well, me."

Amber's response was immediate and visceral. It came accompanied with a small amount of anger, which surprised both of them. "Why would I be turned off kissing you any more than any other person?! You are as worthy of love as anyone else! Condition or no condition, bah. I like you and I wanted to. That should be enough, shouldn't it? And I'll do it again!"

Deep crimson spread over her cheeks and she cleared her throat. "So yeah, um...I'm happy to kiss you in public. Or private. Or whenever the fancy strikes."

Reuben kept his mouth closed as he received his little scolding. "As long as we both enjoy it, then. I would be happy to kiss you whenever or wherever you'd like." He then turned and placed a kiss on Amber's cheek.

Silence fell for a little while as Amber allowed the familiar scenes of *Star Wars* to calm her mind. She ran the fingers of one hand up and down Reuben's sternum, the light pressure against her fingertips relaxing her while she ate with the other. The vampire's cool skin felt good as it pulled the heat of embarrassment away from Amber's body until she felt pleasantly chilled.

When her dinner was finished, Amber re-positioned herself so she lay stretched along the back of the couch with plenty of room for Reuben to be the little spoon if he wished. Little by little she found her eyelids drooping and her breathing slowing until she slipped into a light sleep. She couldn't remember the last time she'd felt this comfortable and content. The fear from earlier had vanished into the void as she snoozed toward the end of the film.

Reuben had no shame as he took the open space in front of Amber. He was a little further down the couch, allowing Amber to watch the movie over his head without obstruction. His attention shifted between the movie and the gorgeous woman behind him.

Before he could drift to sleep, he could feel the soft breath of a sleeping Amber against his hair. With a huge smile on his face, he pulled a blanket over the two of them. The soft rhythm of Amber's heartbeat lulled Reuben to sleep soon after.

*T*he loud music of the closing credits broke the spell and Amber's eyes opened slowly with an accompanying yawn. She felt quite good after her nap. But she felt better opening her eyes to a handsome man who had, despite their time together being so short, become important to her. She smiled and brought Reuben's hand to her lips, brushing each of the vampire's fingertips. "Sorry I fell asleep...that was rather rude of me."

A few indistinguishable mumbles escaped Reuben's lips. He rolled over to bury his head in Amber's chest. His hands tangled themselves in the band t-shirt and tugged the wearer close. He took a deep, relaxed breath. "Yeah, how dare you fall asleep," he murmured, voice gravelly.

"I am going to have to be more disappointing, though," Amber sighed, wrapping her legs around Reuben's waist. "I should go home. It's really late."

Reuben looked up with puppy dog eyes and his arms slipped around Amber's torso. "What if you didn't?"

Truthfully, Amber seriously considered the question for a moment before shaking her head. "I should sleep in my own bed. But what if we went on another date on your next day off? Something romantic, like stargazing?" She began disentangling herself from the vampire despite his soft protests. "You're such a goof."

"Fine. I'll let you go, as long as you promise not to make me wait another week to see you." Reuben released his grip and sat up, his hair sticking up in various directions. "Do you need me to call you a car?"

Amber nodded and began gathering her things while Reuben pulled out his phone. Ten minutes later the car pulled up in front of the house and she gave Reuben a quick kiss on the lips. "Text me your schedule in the morning, okay Benji? I'll see you again soon!"

CHAPTER 23

><><>Mr. DeVito<><><

"*T*he clock is ticking, Reuben. We only have four months left until the election and we still aren't anywhere near the numbers we need." Stella's eyes burned holes through Mr. DeVito's face while her long nails tapped the desk in agitation.

Mr. DeVito fidgeted with the cuff of his sleeve, but maintained eye contact and a straight spine. "I really don't know what else to do, Stella. I've been volunteering even more than usual and it always seems to backfire. Even Amber backfired for a moment, there, but I got her back."

His eyes widened as he realized he hadn't actually told Stella about the bump in the road with the plan. Her face grew cold and he hurried to save himself. "We had a minor disagreement about publicity, but it's resolved now. Nothing to worry about."

"It better not be," Stella replied, sliding a tiny envelope across the desk, "because you may not know what else to do, but I do. This is an invitation to the yearly end-of-summer barbecue put on by *The MB Tribune.* HOME has made a generous sponsorship donation and you are going to attend as our representative. Take that cute girlfriend of yours with you and mingle with the journalists. And for all that is good, just try to act like a normal person for once!"

A sinking feeling filled Mr. DeVito's stomach. *The MB Tribune* was the largest newspaper in the state and held a lot of sway as far as public opinion. Rubbing shoulders with their journalists could definitely give him an advantage if he could win their favor, but... "Isn't this kind of a risky plan, though? If any tiny thing goes wrong, this could blow up in our faces."

Stella waved her hand nonchalantly. "You're not wrong. But the possible benefits outweigh the risks. I have no doubt that you are capable of managing a casual barbecue without getting involved in any fights."

When it was put that way, what argument could he really give that wouldn't make him look like the problem? Mr. DeVito curled his toes in his shoes and nodded. "I understand." He picked up the envelope and removed the invitation, the baseball-themed card announcing the event would be held that Saturday. "I will check with G– er, *Amber* that she is available."

"Good boy," Stella replied, her eyes returning to their usual brightness. "And you should bring Amber to the office sometime. We would all like to meet her."

><><>Reuben<><><

*R*euben held Amber's hand tightly across the center console. He could sense the waves of fear that were rolling off of her. "I promise, Gem. I will be at your side the entire time. Even if you go into the restroom, I'll stand guard outside the door with my eyes and ears at full alert."

The vampire glanced away from the road to look at Amber with comically wide eyes. She laughed and smacked his shoulder playfully. "I'm nervous, but not *that* nervous."

"Good. I really appreciate that you're willing to attend this thing with me, Gem. I know it's our first foray into appearing together publicly and people are going to be watching us. But it's not as high-pressure as the gala will be, so it's a nice entry point." Reuben kissed the back of Amber's hand and pulled into the parking lot.

The event was being held at the baseball diamonds in the middle of town, where the city's major league baseball team practiced. From the lot, Reuben and Amber could see the crowd already milling around the dozens of pop-up canopies where various sponsors had tables. Reuben followed Amber's gaze, chuckling when he realized her eyes were focused intently on the smoke rising from the grills. "Hungry?"

"Starving!" Amber replied, unbuckling her seatbelt and taking a deep breath.

Reuben could see her hands shaking despite the smile on her face. He hurried to open the door for Amber and helped her out, locked the car, and tenderly took one of those shaking hands in his own. "You've got this. You don't have to give your permission for *anyone* to interview you. My job is to schmooze the reporters; yours is just to eat as much as you want and have fun."

"*That* I can definitely handle."

The couple made a bee-line for the barbeque, Amber holding Reuben's hand tightly and her shoulder brushing his. She didn't leave his side even a half step until they reached the buffet table. It was laden with salads, buns, toppings, condiments, and desserts.

While his girlfriend busied herself making a plate, Reuben kept his eyes busy looking for George Bracken. According to Stella, George was their best 'in' for getting a positive article in *The MB Tribune*. Something about his sister in law being a supernatural? Truth be told, Reuben had stopped listening by that point.

Amber piled her plate high and finally stepped away from the line with a beaming grin on her face. *By the gods her smile is so beautiful,* Reuben thought as he led Amber over to an unoccupied table beneath an umbrella. Despite having put on his sunscreen this time, the vampire still did his best to stay out of the sun as much as possible.

"How is the food?" he asked as Amber took a *very* large bite from her hamburger. She chewed a few times and gave him a thumbs-up, her eyes bright with happiness. "Good! That's what I like to hear.

Once you're finished, we can go wander the booths, hm? I'm sure there are lots of door prizes and things you can enter to win if you want to."

Amber swallowed and nodded. "Sure! I do like free things." She took another large bite and Reuben couldn't keep his eyes off her. He sat on his chair with one foot on the chair next to him and his baseball cap pulled down low over his brow. The plain white t-shirt he wore lifted a little, exposing his side just a sliver over the stone-washed blue jeans.

Around the couple, people were definitely staring. Reuben did his best to ignore them in favor of conversing with Amber between bites, the pair laughing at their soft conversation. Nobody approached them at first, instead choosing to gossip.

Until a large, bushy black man with a well-oiled mustache and a twinkle in his eye wandered over with an open can of soda in his hand. "Well, well, well. If it isn't *the* Reuben DeVito. I heard rumors you might be here, and it seems they were right."

Reuben put his foot back on the grass and gestured toward the free chair. "Ah, Mr. Bracken! I had heard rumors about your own fine self." The vampire extended a hand and George shook it cheerfully before taking the offered seat.

"Oh, come now. This is a casual setting, Reuben. Call me George, eh? And who might this lovely little lady be?" George turned that warm smile on Amber, who half-hid her face behind Reuben's back.

"Thank you, George," Reuben replied, wrapping an arm around Amber and pulling her protectively against his side. "This is my girl-friend, Amber. Amber, this is George Bracken."

Amber waved shyly and George began to laugh. It was a deep laugh, rising up from the belly and full of honey. "Nice to meet you, Amber! Never thought I'd see the day that Reuben found himself a girl, but good on you for managing to pull him away from his work. I swear, every time one of my journalists attends anything resembling a charity event, there's Mr. DeVito in the thick of it."

Reuben did his best not to show any signs of embarrassment, but his knee bounced slightly anyway. "Yes, it was certainly unexpected for me, too. But you know how these kinds of things go. Showing up when you least expect it." To calm himself, Reuben rested his cheek against Amber's hair and took a deep breath. She smelled of lilac, green apple, and citrus.

George's glittering eyes missed nothing of the movement, but as far as Reuben could tell, the man didn't seem displeased. "Have you two checked which team you're on yet? This year they named them 'The Pens' and 'The Swords.' Personally, I'll be rooting for the Pens. Everyone knows they're mightier than the sword."

Reuben's left eyebrow raised. "I have no idea what you're talking about…"

"It's tradition!" George exclaimed in exaggerated shock. "Every year, the Falcons split their major league players into two teams, and the other half of each team is made up of the sponsors' representatives who play a single inning each. It's just a fun, casual game of baseball after the barbeque with prizes for the winning team. You and your plus one should be on the same team and the same inning." He gestured toward the *Tribune*'s tent. "The lists are over there."

"Stella neglected to mention that part," Reuben sighed, his eyes darting to the tent and back to George. "Are you sure they want *me* to play? What with my abilities and all?"

George chuckled and took a swig of his soda. "Things are changing, my boy. Slowly, but they are changing. Why don't you go show them that supernaturals can play without cheating? That would make a great headline for the sports section, actually. 'Vampire leads team to victory at *The MB Tribune*'s yearly baseball game!' Who knows? It might help start a discussion about allowing supernaturals back on sports teams."

"What do you think, sweetheart?" Reuben asked, turning to face Amber. "I told you I wouldn't make you do anything you don't want to do, and I meant it."

After a moment of thought, Amber shrugged her shoulders. "I suppose we could play. I can't imagine we're the only ones who won't know what we're doing out there. It might be kind of fun."

"You heard the little lady! We'll see you on the field, Reuben." George gave the couple a wink and sauntered off to find someone else to talk to. Amber and Reuben watched him go with bemused looks on their faces.

Amber finished the rest of her plate and folded it in half. "Well, he was super nice! I rather liked him. Shall we go check the teams before we explore the rest of the booths?"

"Sounds like a plan." Reuben rose and took Amber's hand again to follow her to the trash can. He wasn't as immediately taken by George as Amber was, but it *had* been nice that the man didn't flinch at the handshake or seem the least bit afraid. Reuben had crossed paths with George plenty of times in the past, but never actually took the time to talk to him before today.

Amber pulled Reuben to the *Tribune*'s tent and eagerly scanned the team lists, grinning when she found their names. "Look at that, Benji! They really *did* include us! We're playing for the Swords."

"Good for us," Reuben replied.

CHAPTER 24

><><>**Amber**<><><

*D*espite being the exact opposite of sporty, Amber found herself quite excited about the baseball game. Not to play, really; she actually kept picturing Reuben in a uniform and blushing furiously at the mental image.

She dragged Reuben from booth to booth, staring at all the offerings while feeling safe with her protector. *Two months ago I never would have imagined myself willingly going out in a crowd like this,* she thought, and the grin on her face expanded. *Much less agreeing to play baseball in front of all these people...*

The thought made her anxiety begin to rise again, but Amber gave Reuben's hand a squeeze and replayed his promises in her mind.

"Don't worry. I'll be there the whole time. That trash can of a human is still behind bars and there's no way he'll be there. Your brain is just being unkind to you. And if you get overwhelmed, just let me know and we'll go home."

The crackling sound of a microphone being turned on floated over the crowd and Amber paused to listen. It was a little hard to hear over the buzz of the crowd, but she managed to make out, "The baseball game begins in fifteen minutes! If all players could report to the leader tent, we'll pass out jerseys and get started!"

"We get jerseys?!" Amber exclaimed, practically jumping for joy. Her fantasy was coming true! She pulled Reuben toward the *Tribune*'s tent and the pair got into line, where Reuben stood behind her with his arms draped around her neck like a necklace. When they reached the front of the line, the officiator crossed their names off the list on his clipboard and flipped through the plastic-wrapped jerseys.

"Here you two go," he said with a smile as he handed them over. Reuben reached out over Amber and took both of them before steering her off to the left with his elbows. Their feet were in perfect sync and allowed Reuben to press his chest against Amber's back as they walked out of the way.

Amber tore hers open excitedly, to find the jersey had the number 21 and "Swords" on the back. "They are even personalized!" she laughed, pulling the shirt over her head and allowing it to fall softly down her torso. Reuben nodded and put on his own, number 22.

"Do I look like a baseball player now?" he asked with a laugh. Amber nodded and rose up on her heels to kiss him, her arms wrapped tightly around his chest.

"You sure do. And a very attractive one at that. Come on, let's get over to the dugout! I don't know how fast the first inning is going to go, but we don't want to be late to ours!" Amber grabbed Reuben's hand and again began dragging him through the crowd of people to where the other jersey-ed players were congregating.

In the chaos of it all, nobody really seemed to notice or care that there was a vampire in their midst. Laughter and good-natured banter buzzed around Amber and Reuben, and Amber couldn't help feeling excitement filling up her lungs.

With the shrill screech of a whistle, the game began. Amber led Reuben to the metal grandstands to the right of third base, but rather than sitting she stepped up and gripped the chain link fence. Reuben stood behind her and wrapped his arms around her waist, resting his chin on the top of her head.

"You're doing so well," he whispered in her ear. His breath felt like a crisp autumn breeze on her skin.

Amber dropped one of her hands and rested it on Reuben's. "It helps that people aren't really paying all that much attention to us. And that you are here to keep me safe."

An affirming grunt vibrated Amber's shoulder blades. "Always." The couple watched the entire inning that way: Amber staring through the fence with bright eyes, while Reuben held her protectively in his arms.

"Those playing the second inning, report to your team's dugout! Pens on the left, Swords on the right! The second inning will begin in five minutes!"

Reuben gave Amber a squeeze and released her. "That's us, sweetheart. Time to show them our skills."

"Yours, maybe," Amber replied with a laugh. She stood on her tiptoes and gave Reuben a kiss on the cheek before they started toward the dugout. They weren't far from it, but getting through the crowd proved a bit of a challenge.

The team captain didn't even have to ask their names as they walked up. He scanned Reuben and barely managed to hide the look of disgust on his face. "Ah, DeVito. You and..." he glanced at the clipboard, "Miss Marcus are third and fourth to bat. When we switch to fielders, you'll play left and right fielders."

Amber felt a snowball fill her stomach. She supposed it had been silly of her to expect everyone to be cheerful toward her boyfriend, but at least they were being allowed to play. Plus...they had her name. "Okay, thank you!" she answered more out of a desire to end the conversation than gratitude. She felt Reuben's arm wrap comfortingly around her shoulder and allowed him to push her into the dugout.

Thankfully, the rest of the team didn't seem to mind the vampire's presence. They chatted animatedly amongst themselves while Amber and Reuben sat quietly on the bench with their helmets in their hands.

"Are you going to be okay while I take my turn at bat?" Reuben asked, turning his soft eyes on Amber. "We won't be apart very long."

Amber nuzzled Reuben's shoulder with her cheek and nodded. "I'll be fine," she whispered. "If anything happens, I'll just shout and I know you'll be back here before I can even take another breath." And she *did* know it was true. She could feel it in his touch and see it in his eyes. Reuben wanted this excursion to go perfectly, and he would make sure it did.

"DeVito, you're up."

Reuben stood and headed for home plate, swinging the baseball bat a few times as he walked. Amber's brown eyes were focused intently on him and her stomach once again filled with butterflies. He looked so attractive with his striped jersey and strong shoulders.

She was so focused that it took the person next to her three tries to get her attention. "Hey. Hey. Hey!" the man said, smiling when Amber finally realized she was being spoken to. "Hello! I'm Kyle Zeborski. You must be Mr. DeVito's mysterious girlfriend!"

Amber nodded, but shrunk a little into herself. She didn't particularly like the glimmer in the man's eyes, but without Reuben to run interference, she took a deep breath to calm herself.

Kyle's grin widened. "Well, well! What's it like being a vampire's girlfriend? Does he...you know?" He bared his teeth and snapped his jaw a couple of times.

"Excuse you, no he does not," Amber replied with more force than she expected. "It's no different than dating any other man, aside from the sheer number of people who ask insensitive questions and make rude assumptions!"

Kyle seemed taken aback by the veracity of Amber's response. He leaned back and waved a hand vaguely between them. "I'm sorry, I suppose that *was* rather rude of me. Looks like it's your turn."

He pointed as Reuben hit the ball and sent it flying far over second base. The vampire dropped the bat and began running toward first base at a perfectly human speed. The professional player acting as coach waved Reuben forward as he hit first and he pivoted, making it to second base just before the second baseman caught the ball.

"Good job, sweetheart!" Amber yelled as she stepped up to the plate herself. She also waved the bat a couple of times to feel its weight. It had been easily twenty years since she'd played baseball, but it had been her favorite sport to play (badly) as a child.

Her eyes focused on the pitcher, hands slightly sweaty as he wound up and lobbed the ball in her direction. She swung and felt the end of her bat connect solidly with the ball, catching her off guard.

"Run!" called the coach, and Amber dropped the bat. She began to run, completely ignoring where the ball had ended up or whether it would beat her to the base. Just five feet from first, she tripped over her own foot and fell forward. She looked up and saw the baseball flying toward the first baseman then in front of her, where the base was only a few inches away.

She reached out her hand and placed it on the base just before the baseman caught the ball. "Safe!" called the coach, and a wide grin spread across Amber's face. The baseman offered her a hand and hauled her back to her feet with a smile.

"People don't usually slide into first," he teased, "and they don't usually slide on their bellies, either." He tossed the ball to the pitcher and Amber did her best to hide the redness in her cheeks.

Kyle stepped up to the plate and hit the ball with apparent ease, knocking it deep into the outfield. Amber and Reuben both crossed home plate safely and headed back to the dugout. Once inside, Reuben wrapped Amber in his arms and lifted her off the floor with a laugh. "I was so sure you were going to be out when you tripped," he admitted, then kissed Amber firmly on the lips.

Amber melted into the kiss, forgetting for a moment that the pair were in a *very* public place. Those cool lips felt like a drink from the sweetest spring and she drank them in, eyes closed in pure bliss.

Their team didn't win, but Amber couldn't find it in herself to care. With a belly full of barbeque and a bag full of pens, stickers, and various other branded knicknacks, she danced to the song playing in her head as Reuben led her by the hand back to the car.

"You seem to be quite pleased," Reuben laughed, pulling Amber closer to his side. "I was worried you would spend the entire day as an anxious wreck. But you barely seemed to have any issues at all. I'm proud of you."

Amber beamed as she nodded and gave a little skip. "That is kind of normal for me, actually. I get myself all worked up about being in crowds or being recognized, but once I'm there it's not so bad."

"Good. Maybe someday we'll get you past being anxious at all." Reuben stopped short of the car and fished around for his keys. While waiting, Amber felt her phone buzz in her pocket. She pulled it out to see who was texting her and found that Jade had sent her a link to a news article.

She gave a little sigh and tapped on the link. "Well, so it begins," she said as the page loaded. "Jade sent me a news link. Shall we take bets on what nonsense she thought I needed to read?"

Reuben pressed the unlock button on the key fob and rolled his eyes. "No thank you. I don't want to get into another fight over you reading that stuff." He held Amber's door open and helped her inside before entering his own and turning on the car.

"Annual **Tribune** *Barbeque Huge Success,"* the headline read. Amber scanned the text, finding very little of note other than a mention of Reuben being in attendance and joining the baseball game. At the bottom of the article was a gallery of photos, which she opened out of curiosity.

In the middle of the dozen photos, she found a clear photograph of herself and Reuben kissing. "Oh," Amber groaned, "that's what Jade thought was noteworthy." She turned her phone screen so Reuben could see the picture.

"Not a bad photo," he said, smiling. "That's a pretty cute couple, there. I might have to save that picture to my phone. How was the article?"

Amber shrugged and put the phone back in her pocket. "You were barely more than a footnote. But it was a positive footnote, so I guess there's that?" She took Reuben's hand and rubbed his chilly palm on her sunburnt cheek. "I should have put on sunscreen like you told me to..."

"Admitting I was right about something this early in the relationship? Wow. Better watch out that you don't set a dangerous precedent." Reuben winked and both of them began to laugh, feeling completely at peace after a wonderful day together.

CHAPTER 25

><><>**Amber**<><><

The next day, Amber had agreed to meet Reuben for a little more private date. "I'll be there in about fifteen minutes, okay? Make sure you bring a jacket in case it gets cold."

She laughed and closed the bedroom door behind her with her toes, her phone on speaker with Reuben in one hand and a pair of pants in the other. "You sound like an old mother hen, Benji. It's barely the end of summer and there's not a single cloud predicted tonight. I don't need a jacket. I'm headed out the door now and I'll meet you at Tres Leches in fifteen."

"Fine, but don't come complaining to me when you're a freezing chicky and I can't do anything to warm you up. I'll see you soon."

The evening air was pleasant as Amber took a deep breath and walked across the parking lot to the bus stop. Yes, she could have saved a fare by letting Reuben pick her up at her apartment. But even though the comments on all the articles about yesterday's barbeque had been positive, she still hadn't quite shaken the fear of her address getting out. So, an evening rendezvous it was. She raised her hand to shade her eyes from the setting sun and, seeing the bus trundling down the road, picked up her pace.

She made it onto the bus without issue and upon arrival, spotted Reuben's shiny black car sitting in the empty lot across the street from the cafe. It reflected the setting sun, turning it into a glittering array of reds and oranges. Amber hopped out of the bus and ran across the street with a wide grin on her face. "Benji!" she exclaimed, waving as she went.

The door swung open and Reuben stepped out with an equally big smile, arms extended for a hug. Amber barreled right into his chest and wrapped her arms around him. Her nose buried in his shirt, she drank in the scent of vanilla and sandalwood. He towered over her and she felt like the rest of the world had been blocked out by his form.

"You ready for our adventure?" Reuben asked as he walked Amber to the passenger side door and opened it for her. "We have a bit of a drive, first, but I think you'll like our destination when we get there."

Amber climbed into the car and buckled the seatbelt. "That's fine. I'm excited to see this mysterious place, though. Are you sure you can't give me any clues?" She batted her eyelashes at Reuben, but he remained strong and settled into the driver's seat. Amber pouted, but reached across the center console and grabbed Reuben's hand. "You're such a brat."

"I'll take it," Reuben teased. He eased the car onto the road and headed south, away from city center and toward the countryside. As they drove, Reuben stroked Amber's hand with his thumb and hummed along to the radio.

Amber leaned back in her seat and watched the buildings go by. Streetlights blurred in the corner of her eye, but grew farther and farther apart. "We're going out to the middle of nowhere?"

"You can't see the stars properly in the city," Reuben replied with a glitter in his eye. "They'll be much more impressive where we're going. Don't worry. I wouldn't take you anywhere dangerous."

"I know." And she did. Amber yawned and her eyes closed; soon she had drifted away. Next she knew, the sound of gravel under their tires and the bumpiness of the road woke her back up. It was completely dark, now; all she could see was the space illuminated by their headlights.

Reuben looked over as Amber stirred and brushed the hair out of her face. "Good morning, Sleeping Beauty. I hope your nap means you won't fall asleep on me while we're trying to be romantic."

Amber opened her mouth to protest that she always slept in cars, but just then Reuben slowed and stopped beneath a tree. She looked around curiously, blinking in an attempt to get her eyes to adjust faster to the darkness.

"Want to help me get the stuff out of the back?" Reuben pressed the button on his key fob that opened the hatch back, opened Amber's door for her, and then followed her around the car. He picked up the picnic basket and handed her the blanket. Amber took it and tucked it under her arm, then grabbed Reuben's hand.

He led her away from the gravel parking area, past a small grove of trees, and onto a field of soft grass. The pair walked about fifty yards away from the car before Reuben stopped and set down the basket. "I think this will be a good spot."

Amber nodded and shook open the blanket. "Help me get it flat?" she asked, less because she needed assistance and more because it meant Reuben had to take a few steps closer to her. She watched the way his muscles rippled under his tight-fitting polo as they spread the blanket and sat down next to each other.

"I've never been out this far," she said, looking around at the waving grass and dark shadows of trees in the distance. The full moon actually made it quite bright now that her eyes were adjusting. She could at least see all the important things: the stars, and Reuben's face. "Where are we, anyway?"

"Buena Park." Reuben flipped open the picnic basket and handed Amber a neatly-wrapped package of fancy chocolates. "I used to come here all the time when I was a kid. It used to have a playground and ball field back in the eighties, but about fifteen years ago it was all torn down. Hardly anyone comes out here anymore, so we're perfectly safe."

It suddenly struck Amber that she had no idea how old Reuben actually was. She opened her mouth to ask, only to suddenly wonder if that was a rude question to ask a vampire. Even ruder than asking a woman, she'd assume? And they were already just regaining their footing together. Instead she unwrapped one of the chocolates and occupied her mouth with that.

"You like those? I wasn't sure what kind of chocolates are your favorite, so I asked my coworkers and bought the most popular ones."

Amber nodded, her chest feeling like her heart had expanded to overfill the space. "That's the sweetest thing a guy has ever done for me. Whoever actually gets your heart is going to be a lucky person." She re-tied the bag and placed it on the blanket next to her, leaning back and supporting herself with her hands. "And it's super cute that you brought me somewhere from your childhood. It's like you're fulfilling every romance trope."

"I *am* supposed to be giving you material for your book," Reuben replied. "And I did warn you that cheesy romances were my only point of reference as far as being a good boyfriend." He lay back completely and folded his arms behind his head, his eyes taking in the vastness of the stars.

Amber scooted closer to him with laughter on her lips. "I suppose you did tell me that. I just seemed to forget somewhere along the way." *There are a lot of things I seemed to forget along the way...like the fact that I wasn't supposed to actually fall in love with you.*

><><>**Reuben**<><><

*R*euben leaned back and watched a small cloud as it drifted across the north star. Despite how happy he felt to be spending more time with his now-favorite person, anxiety gnawed on his stomach and burned in his throat. He knew the conversation he had planned for tonight would not be easy, even if he took her to the first place he had ever felt truly safe.

But things were getting out of hand, and there were a few things Amber needed to know before they went any further. "Amber, I-" Reuben went to run a hand through his hair, forgot he had a hat on, and adjusted the cap instead.

He stole a glance at his gorgeous date in the moonlight. Amber looked like a tempting mirage, which was fitting in his situation. Something that looked so real, but would disappear the second he got too close. She tilted her head and wrapped her arm around his, encouraging him to continue.

Reuben took another breath to calm himself and said, "I feel like I need to be more honest with you. I can't help noticing that you keep making these romantic gestures that feel entirely real. I don't mind; in fact, I actually rather like it. But I want you to know more about me before we slip past the point of no return."

Reuben watched Amber's face for a reaction, expecting to get a dose of fear. Instead, Amber's eyes softened and she wrapped both hands around Reuben's. "I would love to know more about you, Reuben. You can tell me anything, I promise."

Everything about her response was so genuine that Reuben felt the ice encasing his heart give a distinct *crack*.

"If you're sure, then. I'll spare you the grisly early details, but about ten years ago I found myself slumped against a brick wall at the entrance to an alleyway in the outer city limits. I hadn't eaten in nearly six weeks because the homes of vampires I usually robbed in the suburbs had gotten better security systems. My mind was gone with starvation, Amber. I couldn't think in full sentences anymore.

"I had made a vow back when I was turned that I would never attack a human being no matter the circumstances, but as I sat there, I was so close. So close to breaking that vow. I would have rather died, but vampires can't starve to death." Reuben's tone grew bitter and he clenched his teeth as the memory enveloped him like a cold fog.

Amber tightened her grip; Reuben took a breath and continued. "The only thing that saved me was a werewolf named Bryce. He happened by at the last possible moment and carried me to his house. He fed me, clothed me, and introduced me to HOME."

Amber scooted a little closer and tucked her arm under Reuben's before again taking his hand. The pair sat silently for a few moments while Reuben gathered his thoughts and Amber stroked his palm. "Go on," she coaxed, voice soft as dandelion down.

"HOME changed my life," Reuben whispered. "Thanks to them, I have a house. I have food. I have safety. After thirty years of surviving on the streets, I have stability. And Amber? I would do *anything* to keep that stability.

"But HOME is at a critical juncture. We are doing what we can to keep our brothers and sisters safe, but we don't have the funds to keep this up if we have to start paying lawyers to fight for us. We would have to lower the food bank budget which keeps vampires sane, or lower the production of shifter medication which allows werewolves to live normal lives."

"Which would only result in more attacks, more lawsuits, and more money being reallocated," Amber said with a sigh. The picture was becoming incredibly clear, and it wasn't a pretty one. It was a vicious cycle with little control to be had.

Reuben nodded sadly and looked back up at the heavens. "I'm afraid, Amber. When you strip away the title and suit, I'm a vampire who has seen how frail my existence is. If HOME fails, who knows how long I could keep my vow? I feel terrible dragging you into this, but I am so glad I met you. Even though you should be running as fast as you can in the opposite direction."

"Rubbish!" Amber shouted, her sudden outburst causing Reuben to jump. "You have *me* now, and I would not let you fall. And I can't be the only human on this planet who can see past the end of my own nose! Just keep doing what you're doing and I have no doubt that you'll be able to impact generations to come."

She turned those fiery eyes on Reuben and continued a little more softly. "Your image is spotless. We'll get you elected. Then you can be the hope others like you are searching for."

Reuben rolled over and tucked his face into his arms as shame threatened to overcome him. How could he get Amber to understand that he wasn't some saint? That the least of his sins was dragging this angel of a human into a facade that could end up hurting her deeply?

And how could he tell her about the very real danger he was in? That *she* could be in, by extension?

Amber lifted Reuben's chin gently and stared into his eyes. "Benji. Just because bad things happened to you in the past doesn't mean that you were tainted by them. Look at all of the amazing things you have accomplished since then! Think of all the supernaturals whose lives are better because of *you. My* life is better because of you."

A single tear leaked from the corner of Reuben's eye and Amber gently brushed it away. "I mean it, Benji. I already tried running away, and it was the worst week of my life. I don't care what *almost* happened a decade ago. I care what is happening right *now.*"

This human! Reuben shouted inside his skull. She was reckless and she was naive. But she was also kind and loving and beautiful. With his heart threatening to cut off his windpipe, Reuben rolled to his side and pulled Amber against his body. He wrapped his arms around her torso and his legs around hers like an octopus as he buried his face in her hair. Her back felt hot against his chest and her heartbeat pounded in his ears.

He couldn't help feeling guilty about opening up. He didn't want Amber to feel bad for him. That wasn't the plan! He'd never wanted to burden anyone else with his problems, much less the person who had started to thaw his unbeating heart. But it also felt so freeing to admit his darkest moment and still have her by his side.

And he didn't want this to end. Laying in the fragrant grass, staring at the stars and holding Amber felt *right.* He was glad this wasn't some dream that disappeared the second he opened his eyes. She was in front of him. She was *real.* There was a woman on this earth that could look past Reuben's unfortunate situation and see more than a pair of fangs.

"I need to tell you one more thing." Reuben sat up and wrapped his arms around his knees. His voice betrayed his fear and Amber reached out to take his hand. "And I don't want you to freak out, promise?"

"I don't like the sound of that, Benji."

Reuben clenched his eyes and gave Amber's hand a squeeze. "I... haven't just been dodging the paparazzi. Remember how I mentioned dodging the protestors too that day I was late to the cafe? Well, it's because some of the more radical protestors have decided 'peaceful' isn't enough."

He paused, the words unwilling to unstick themselves from his throat. Amber stared at him with worry dotting her eyes like stars. "There have been attempts on my life," he finally managed. "But it's okay! I've been extra careful and nobody has even come close to succeeding."

"Attempts on your life? Like...*recent* assassination attempts?"

Reuben nodded and Amber's worry tinted black with anger. "Why didn't you tell me?" she shouted. "Why haven't I seen anything on the news? Have they been caught? What happened? Weren't we in danger yesterday, spending all day out in public?!"

"Hey, hey. Take a breath." Reuben stroked Amber's cheek until her taut muscles somewhat relaxed. "Some of them have been caught, yes. But due to the circumstances, it seems like there's someone higher up directing them. And the police haven't caught that person yet. So far the details haven't been leaked to the media, thankfully. That's why you didn't know. And there was so much security following us yesterday that nothing could have actually happened. They were just undercover."

Amber sat in silence for so long that Reuben began to worry that she was about to dump him again. But she finally wrapped her arms around his chest and buried her face in his back. "You are going to be safe though, right? These people can't actually hurt you?"

As guilty as he felt about it, Reuben lied. "You are right. I'll be perfectly fine."

Reuben tilted his head up and kissed the bottom of Amber's chin, desperate to change the topic before she started asking any more questions. "You know, it's getting pretty late." His hands traveled up her t-shirt and snaked farther around Amber's body. "A rideshare will be a little more expensive than usual." He placed another kiss on Amber's chin, a little closer to her throat this time. "It's not safe for such a pretty woman to be out at night by herself."

He was using every excuse in the book, working himself up to making Amber a risky offer. "You could spend the night at my house. Plus, I could drive us to our favorite coffee shop in the morning."

"I'm not worried about any of that," she murmured, wrapping her arms around Reuben and tangling her fingers in his hair. "I'm happy to share another cup of something hot with you. Though...I didn't bring anything to change into. I don't know how well I'll sleep in jeans."

Reuben was ready to come up with an excuse for anything Amber replied with. Clothing was an easy one. "It's okay. If you need a set of clothes, I'm sure I could find something in my closet for you to wear." The idea of Amber wearing his clothing gave Reuben good shivers, but his foggy brain didn't linger on it.

Amber poked Reuben teasingly and closed her eyes. "I think I'll stay, then. It's probably going to be unpleasant outside soon or something. Maybe it will start to snow. Insert your own excuse here." She yawned widely and allowed her neck to relax, dropping her head onto Reuben's chest.

CHAPTER 26

><><>**Amber**<><><

*I*t was nearly midnight when Reuben's garage door closed and the car expelled two love drunk idiots. Their hands refused to part as they entered the house, removed their shoes, and made their way up the stairs toward the living room.

"Let me go find you something to change into," Reuben said while undoing the buttons of his polo and heading for the bedroom door. Amber nodded and flopped onto his couch, yawning widely. She barely had time to get comfortable before he returned with a t-shirt and some sweatpants. "These are probably too big, but should be fine for sleeping."

Amber took the clothes and disappeared into the bathroom for a few minutes. When she returned, she saw that Reuben had brought out some bedding just in case she didn't feel comfortable sleeping in his bed yet. Which was completely fair; she wasn't. He'd wrapped himself in a fluffy duvet and waited, eyes focused on the bathroom door.

Reuben stifled a chuckle and Amber shot him a dirty look. The clothes were easily four sizes too big and probably looked silly, but they were comfortable. He held open his arms and she stumbled over, happily dropping into his lap and resting her head in the hollow of his neck. He wrapped them both in the blanket and gave Amber a squeeze. Her body heat soon made the shared space nice and toasty, and Amber's eyelids began to droop.

Their physical proximity seemed to have the opposite effect on the vampire. Wide-eyed, he brushed Amber's hair away from her face. "Can I kiss you again?" he breathed.

"I will happily accept a kiss from such a handsome man," Amber replied sleepily, repositioning her arms around Reuben's torso and pressing their lips together as she pulled him in tightly.

Suddenly, nothing else in the world mattered. At that moment, Reuben wasn't a politician or a vampire. Amber wasn't some girl who made a deal. Her entire existence was Reuben. Their eyes closed as their lips connected. Fire and ice fought desperately, yet moved in a synchronized dance.

Reuben stretched out along the couch and rolled over so Amber lay parallel to him under the blankets. Their lips never left each other as the maneuver was completed. The vampire's hands were a bit too brave as his fingers slipped under Amber's shirt. His thumbs carefully rubbed the warm skin of her stomach and hips.

Amber leaned into the sensation, allowing her shirt to slip up and reveal her stomach and lower back. Her own hands found their way into Reuben's hair, tangling and ensnaring until they provided a solid anchor for Amber to press their lips more firmly together.

She shouldn't be here. She shouldn't be doing this. Nothing they had done the last few days could be justified. This wasn't for their arrangement anymore. She was doing this completely out of need. A soft hum escaped Amber's throat as she leaned up into the kiss again, pushing harder into his lips. She wanted to be closer to Reuben any way he could.

Pulling his face away only an inch to speak, Reuben's cool breath tickled her lips. "Gem..." Reuben gulped. He couldn't speak. "I don't think I'm faking it..."

Reuben's voice was low and riddled with anxiety. Amber ran her fingers gently over his brow in an attempt to smooth out the worry lines. And she blushed. Her nickname, that sweet current of sound uttered only by *her* Reuben, filled the space between them. The confession seemed to strike like lightning in the most tender places of Amber's heart, causing it to threaten to cease its beating.

Her eyes opened wide and slipped desperately into the pools of Reuben's irises and Reuben's into hers, each drowning in the depths of those dark waters. Before Amber could connect her lips back to her mouth, they began to part. "You...I...Benji, I haven't been completely faking from the moment you held my hand. I want...I want you to be mine, and me to be yours. For real. I want you to kiss me like this forever. I want to feel your cool skin against my body and see your face when I wake up in the morning!

"I know it's only been like...a couple of months. But Benji, I want this to be real. Consequences or not, I want you to take me as your own. I can't imagine seeing another person holding your hand or looking your way. Is that selfish? Because if I could rewind time, I would go back to that event and I would ask you to the coffee shop as a real date. I would kiss you first in the rippling blue light of the shark tank. I would introduce you as the only person I've ever loved to my sister at Tres Leches.

"Thank everything that I've only missed such a short period of time while convincing myself this is all pretend! I would take back every last moment that we've lost in this silly deal and drink the fire."

><<>Reuben<><><

*R*euben responded with enthusiasm. It had been so long. *So long* since someone was willing to look past what had happened to him. What he'd become. So long since someone wanted to sit with him. Hold his hand. Rest their head on his shoulder. Kiss him.

And so he kissed her again, inhaling Amber's breath until she broke away, desperate for air. They parted only long enough for a single inhale before jumping back in. Her body heat continued soaking into Reuben's chilled flesh, making him feel almost human against her hands.

Amber's confession lingered in the air, hot and passionate. Reuben could hear her heart pounding like it was going to burst right through her chest as she lowered her head and pressed her forehead into his chest.

He felt like *he* was the one living a romance novel now. The words that Amber spoke sounded genuine and meaningful. His mouth had popped open sometime during Amber's dreamy confession and left him entirely speechless. He clicked his jaw closed and took the deepest breath of his life. Mainly because Amber's hands had slipped to his hips.

But he couldn't find enough brain cells to speak. Reuben instead pulled Amber to him with both hands and gently bit her lower lip.

As the kissing again grew more passionate, Amber rolled over onto her back while Reuben knelt over her, hands on either side of the human's head. He felt an intense burning in his chest, an emotion so unfamiliar that he didn't have a word for it. In response, his irises took on the burning red glow of lava. He didn't notice the change in the heat of the moment; his buzzing brain had him clueless until he caught a glimpse of his reflection in Amber's eyes.

It wasn't the clearest picture in the world, but his red irises stood in high contrast to his pale skin. Reuben froze in place. No, that couldn't be right! His thirst was completely under control! Would Amber be frightened if she saw? He took a deep breath to corral his wild emotions. Now was not the time to get so worked up that he slipped into one of his traumatic flashbacks like he did the night of the soup kitchen brawl, but he could already see the edges of his vision darkening.

He couldn't have one of those episodes in front of Amber! She had only just begun to trust him, and the state of his shredded couch pillows after he came back to himself last time proved he wasn't always trustworthy when they struck. But his breath proved useless. He fell into darkness anyway as his girlfriend's face shifted to the terrified face of a drunken stranger on the street.

The rain was cold on his skin. He could smell the human's fear and hear his pounding heart. All around him were dark streets and the cries of starving vampires. His own throat burned desperately and he clawed at it as if to rip it out. The sting of torn flesh barely registered over the screaming hunger which demanded that he find prey.

And then the human stumbled by, inebriated and unaware of the danger lurking only one shadow over. Instinct took over and Reuben leapt at the man, knocking him to the wet pavement with ease. The human's heartbeat echoed like war drums in the vampire's ears as his fangs extended and he pinned his prey, leaning forward to pierce the thin skin covering the juicy jugular vein.

Their eyes met for the briefest moment. Panic and primal fear clouded the human's face, filling his being so that it strangled his vocal cords and rendered him incapable of screaming. Reuben paused as he momentarily regained a modicum of control, but his desperation soon dragged him under another wave.

He could feel the warm skin against his fangs when suddenly he was yanked backwards. Strong, furred arms pinned his arms to his sides and he was carried away into the darkness. The werewolf was speaking to him, but Reuben was too deep in the throws of terror to make any sense of the words. All he could do was claw at his throat and his captor's arms in a vain attempt to gain control.

CHAPTER 27

><><>**Amber**<><><

"What's the matter?" Amber murmured when the kissing came to an abrupt halt. Her partner's muscles stiffened and she opened her eyes. "Benji? Did I do something wrong? I know I'm not very experienced with this stuff, but-"

Then she saw the change in Reuben's irises and the words froze in her throat. She took a breath to clear them and tilted her head slightly, leaning forward to get a better look. "Well that's different! You didn't warn me your eyes would start to glow." She smiled and wrapped her arms around Reuben's neck, but something was wrong. He didn't react in the slightest.

"Benji? Hello, this is a weird spin on making out." She released his neck and snapped her fingers a couple of times, surprised when he continued staring *through* her with those fiery eyes. "Hey. Reuben? You're starting to freak me out."

She placed both hands on Reuben's chest to push him back, and suddenly he stopped gazing into space and focused on *her*. Some primeval survival instinct activated as the eyes of a hunter stared hungrily into her soul. She had seen that look before...on the night Ryan broke in and attempted to murder her. That look spelled *danger*.

Her pupils dilated. Every muscle in her body screamed to run. Reuben's weight, so comforting just moments before, became claustrophobic. "Reuben, this isn't funny. Knock it off!"

Reuben bared his fangs and she let out a shrill scream. She began struggling in earnest as an accompanying snarl caused her to scream even louder. He began scratching at his neck and Amber pushed him hard, squirming and kicking to break free until Reuben fell to the floor with a thud.

No sooner had she been released than she began gathering her things. Her eyes never left the vampire, who sat on the floor muttering "no, no, no," while occasionally clawing at his throat.

Some small part of her considered figuring out what was going on, but that voice was quickly hushed by the panic screaming *run. Run. RUN.* She stuffed her keys and her phone in her pocket, then noticed her little notebook laying on the floor. Amber snatched it up and shoved it in her pocket as well. With one more glance at Reuben she rushed down the stairs, pausing only to grab her shoes before bursting into the dark neighborhood.

She had run a full block before calming down enough to stop and put her shoes on her feet. Tears streamed down her face, but Amber didn't even notice them as she glanced back repeatedly to ensure she wasn't being followed. She was only aware of her hands shaking as she pulled out her notebook and began rubbing the corner of the cover while running another block. The refillable book had always been a crutch of sorts; the familiar texture of the leather as she ran her fingers over it usually helped ground her during a panic attack.

But these pages brought her no comfort. One by one Amber ripped them out. They fell like autumn leaves to the ground and when the last one settled, she pulled out her phone and dialed the first person she could think of.

The phone only rang twice before being picked up, and Amber didn't even wait to hear a hello. "Jade. I need you to come get me," she sobbed, the words barely coherent. She ran the remaining distance to the neighborhood exit, leaving the torn pages scattered on the sidewalk.

The guard gave Amber a concerned look as she ran through the pedestrian access gate still in clothes far too big for her, but she didn't bother to even wave. Jade screeched up fifteen minutes later and Amber climbed inside, wiping her snotty nose on Reuben's shirt as she slammed the car door behind her.

"Do you want to talk about it?" Jade asked as she put the car in drive and sped back toward town. "What did he do to you? Do I need to go whip some ass? You aren't hurt, are you?" When no answers were immediately forthcoming, Jade pulled some baby wipes from the center console and handed them to Amber. "Here, at least wipe your face. You're staying at my house tonight, okay?"

Amber accepted the wipes and reached out for Jade's hand. Jade held her sister's fingers tightly all the way to her house, only letting go to put the car in park. They sat in silence for a long time, neither of them making any moves to exit the car.

"You were right about him," Amber finally whispered, pulling her feet up onto the seat and burying her face in her knees. "He's a predator. I could see it in his eyes! It was the same hungry look Ryan had when he broke into my bedroom."

Jade grimaced and reached for Amber's hand again. "Hey. Listen to me. I know where your brain is going to go, but you're safe, okay? Ryan is still locked up, and if this scrawny vampire man comes anywhere close to this house, Jeremy will rip him apart. So no nightmares."

"As if saying 'no nightmares' would actually keep them away," Amber replied with a sniffle and a hiccup. "But thanks for the effort."

"That's what older sisters are for." Jade playfully bumped her shoulder into Amber's and removed the keys from the ignition. "How about we go inside and play some Super Smash Bros? I'll make some cocoa and you can take everything out on Ganondorf. And I won't even make you go to bed at a decent hour."

Amber finally smiled and gave her sister a hug across the center console. "Alright, deal."

>‹›‹›Reuben‹›‹›‹

*R*euben returned to a hard floor and an eerie silence. He shivered and stretched the cramps out of his arms and legs, blinking as his brain rebooted little by little. The duvet on the couch clued him in that his evening hadn't been a dream, but even in his altered state he realized that he didn't hear the sound of Amber's breathing.

He hauled himself up from the floor and began searching his house, hoping against hope that he would find Amber hiding in the bathroom or one of the spare bedrooms. But as soon as he descended the stairs and saw his front door hanging wide open, Reuben put on his slippers and hurried out into the night after her.

"Amber?" he called, his keen eyes and ears searching the darkness for any sign of her. A sign which came in the form of a sheet of paper that floated toward him on a soft breeze. Reuben leaned down and picked it up, immediately recognizing the handwriting. Despite being unable to make out half the words, he did recognize his name and could read a single line at the bottom of the page, surrounded in hearts.

I think I love him.

There, in the middle of the sidewalk, Reuben fell to his knees and let out an anguished cry. The paper still in his hand crinkled as his fingers curled into a tight fist and he stared at the stars. Once the initial shock wore off, he gathered the rest of the torn pages, tenderly lining them up as if putting them back together would undo what he had done.

She must have seen his eyes. Surely that was it, right? Surely he didn't... "What have I done?" he murmured over and over, smoothing the wrinkled page like he was trying to calm a crying child. "Did I hurt her? I better not have hurt her!"

Reuben buried his face in his hands, crumpling the torn page against his face. What was he going to do now? He had come so far, only to lose himself the very first time they jumped into the deep end! Only to prove he was dangerous. Only to ruin the first chance for real love he'd had in decades.

No.

No, he couldn't give up that easily. They had come too far to just let her disappear into the night without even trying to make it right. This was *not* going to become another page in his book of failures! He pounded his fist into the sidewalk and looked up, setting his jaw. There had to be a way to fix this. Even if he had to knock on every door in Beaumont to find her and apologize ten thousand times, this was *not* how he would lose Amber Jane Marcus, the light of his life.

ABOUT THE AUTHOR

With a passion for storytelling that began in childhood, Ashley is so proud to finally have something to show for it.

Raised on long-held family land in middle-of-nowhere, Utah, Ashley discovered a love for literature at the age of six, sparked by her dad bringing home Harry Potter before anyone had even heard of it. This early exposure to fantasy (and a healthy dose of competition with her classmates) led to a dream of becoming an author from a young age.

When not immersed in the world of writing, Ashley enjoys playing the piano, singing, gardening, and playing the occasional video game. She currently resides in Southern Utah with her husband and small menagerie.

instagram.com/achapmanwrites
tiktok.com/@ashleychapmanwrites

www.ingramcontent.com/pod-product-compliance
Lightning Source LLC
Chambersburg PA
CBHW032005240626
47153CB00003B/1128